mary-kateandashley

Sweet 16

Look for these

Sweet 16

titles:

1 Never Been Kissed
2 Wishes and Dreams
3 The Perfect Summer
4 Getting There
5 Starring You and Me
6 My Best Friend's Boyfriend

mary-kateandashley

Sweet 16

PLAYING GAMES

Eliza Willard

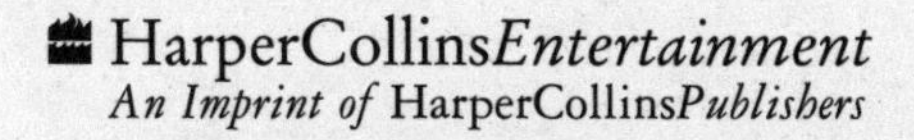

HarperCollins*Entertainment*
An Imprint of HarperCollins*Publishers*

A PARACHUTE PRESS BOOK

A PARACHUTE PRESS BOOK
Parachute Publishing, LLC
156 Fifth Avenue
Suite 325
NEW YORK
NY 10010

First published in the USA by HarperEntertainment 2002
First published in Great Britain by HarperCollins*Entertainment* 2005
HarperCollins*Entertainment* is an imprint of HarperCollins*Publishers* Ltd,
77-85 Fulham Palace Road, Hammersmith, London W6 8JB

SWEET 16 books are created and produced by Parachute Press, LLC, in cooperation with Dualstar Publications, a division of Dualstar Entertainment Group, LLC, published by HarperEntertainment, an imprint of HarperCollins Publishers.

The HarperCollins *Children's Books* website address is
www.harpercollinschildrensbooks.co.uk

1

ISBN 0 00 718099 3

Printed and bound in Great Britain by Clays Ltd, St Ives plc

chapter one

"Mary-Kate Olsen—photojournalist!" Lauren declared. "These pictures look so professional!"

"Thanks," I said. "It's easy when I have great subjects like you three."

I was wandering through the annual Bayside High Art Show with my twin sister, Ashley, and our best friends, Lauren Glazer and Brittany Bowen. Lauren loomed over us, pale and freckle-faced, with wavy brown hair. Brittany was tall, too, and long-legged, with smooth brown skin, dark brown eyes, and short curly hair.

I'd entered some of my photos in the art show—just casual shots taken of Ashley and my friends—and won first place!

Brittany laughed and pointed at a picture of Ashley. "That's *got* to be my favorite," she said.

The photo showed Ashley in her pajamas, bleary-eyed, her wavy blond hair mussed up, having just woken up one morning. I thought she looked adorable. I don't think Ashley agreed with me, though.

Ashley gasped when she saw it. "Mary-Kate!" she cried. "I can't believe you used that one! Now the whole school has seen me in my pajamas!"

"Get over it, Ashley," Brittany said. "Look what she did to *me*." She nodded at a group shot of the four of us, taken with the timer device on my camera. Lauren, Ashley, and I were smiling normally, but Brittany was making a funny, cross-eyed face. "That little joke has come back to haunt me—big time," she added.

"But I love that one!" Lauren exclaimed. "It's so funny!"

"And it's so *us*," Ashley added. "Kind of cool, kind of goofy . . ."

"That's what I was going for," I explained. "The real us, warts and all."

"Speak for yourself, Mary-Kate," Brittany joked. "I don't have warts!"

"Congratulations, Mary-Kate." Someone tapped my shoulder. I turned and found myself face-to-face with my ex-boyfriend, Jake Impenna.

"Hi, Jake," I said. I hadn't spoken to him in a while, not since we broke up. I was so mad at him! He thought I was spending too much time with a friend of mine, Sam McHugh, and got jealous. I couldn't convince him that Sam and I were just friends. I saw a side of Jake I didn't know was there before—and I didn't like it. So we fought about it and broke up. But now that I had cooled off a little, I had to admit I missed him.

"Your pictures are fantastic," Jake said. "Really amazing."

"Thanks," I said.

"You're really talented," he added. "Your photos are the best thing in the art show. Everyone is talking about them."

I melted into a smile. I didn't know what to say. I wanted to tell him I missed him. But I didn't.

"Well—I just wanted to say congratulations." Jake nodded at me and walked away.

Ashley studied my face. "Are you okay?"

"Yeah," I said. "That was nice of him."

"He wasn't just being nice," Ashley insisted. "Everything he said was true. Your pictures *are* the best thing in the art show."

"Well, they did bring me some good luck," I admitted.

"What do you mean?" Lauren asked.

"Ms. Barbour saw my photos when I was hanging them this morning—" I began. Ms. Barbour was a new English teacher.

"What was she like?" Brittany interrupted me. "She's so chic, I'm almost afraid to talk to her. Did you know she used to work for a fashion magazine in New York?"

I nodded. None of us had Ms. Barbour for English, but we'd all noticed her. She didn't really look like a teacher. She was tall and thin, with short, glossy dark hair, funky red glasses, and a closet full of fashionable clothes.

"What did she say?" Lauren asked.

"She's starting up a new school Website," I said. "And she wants me to work on it!"

"That's great!" Brittany exclaimed.

"Excellent!" Ashley slapped me five. "This calls for a celebration. Anybody up for an iced mocha at Click?"

"Let's go," Lauren said.

"Four tall iced mochas," I ordered.

"With extra cocoa on mine," Mary-Kate put in.

"And whipped cream on mine," Lauren said.

Malcolm, who worked behind the counter at Click Café, looked up from the book he was reading. I couldn't help peeking at the title—*Down the Bunny Trail: The Meaning of Rabbits in British Literature.* He was always reading some kind of weird book or journal—everything from cooking magazines to carpentry guides to Roman history. "I have wide interests," he told me once. No kidding.

"Um, I'm sorry, Ashley," Malcolm drawled in his slow, lazy voice. "I totally did not hear what you said."

We repeated our orders. Malcolm swiped his lank brown hair out of his eyes and went to make the coffees. He was skinny and pale, with sleepy eyes.

Mary-Kate, Lauren, Brittany, and I settled at a table near the window. Click Café was my favorite hangout. It was a coffeehouse for teens, and it felt like a private clubhouse for me and my friends.

Malcolm delivered four tall iced mochas to our table. "If you need anything else just yell," he said. "But only if it's really important, okay?"

"Here's to Mary-Kate," Lauren said, clinking her glass against Mary-Kate's.

"All right," Brittany cheered, lifting her glass. "Congrats on your success at the art show!"

"Thanks, you guys." Mary-Kate grinned and sipped her drink.

"So what is this new Website about?" Lauren asked Mary-Kate.

"Ms. Barbour wants it to be like an alternative to the school newspaper," Mary-Kate explained. "I'll help design the Web pages, choose photos, and write captions for them—and maybe write some articles, too."

"Sounds fun," Brittany said.

"And it will look great on your record when you apply to colleges," Lauren added.

"The cool thing is, we're starting it from scratch," Mary-Kate said. "We can make it anything we want it to be! I'm thinking of starting a feature called 'Sixteen'—stuff about what it's like to be sixteen, the fun parts and the hard parts, what different sixteen-year-olds are thinking about . . ."

"I love it!" Lauren gushed. Lauren could always be counted on to be sweet and enthusiastic. "You can interview your friends!"

"Speaking of sixteen," I cut in, "somebody's six-teenth birthday is coming up."

Our eyes turned to Brittany.

"Two weeks from Friday, right, Britt?" Lauren asked.

Brittany smiled and nodded. "It's no big deal," she said.

"No big deal!" I cried. "You're turning sixteen! It changes everything! Doesn't it, Mary-Kate?"

"It's life-altering," Mary-Kate agreed. "The driver's license alone is huge."

"Since you're not having a party, what are your plans?" Lauren asked. "We've got to celebrate some-how!"

Brittany's parents couldn't throw her a big party this year because her mother was pregnant—and the baby was due right around Brittany's birthday.

"Mom said I could have a small dinner party at our house the night of my birthday," Brittany said. "Just the girls—my three best friends. Will you come?"

Mary-Kate nodded. "We'll be there," I promised.

"Definitely," Lauren said. "It sounds like fun. Low-key, just the buds."

"Exactly," Brittany agreed. "But my seventeenth birthday will be the party of the century!" She glanced at the clock on the wall. "I'd better go. French test tomorrow."

She sipped the last of her drink and got up to leave. "See you all tomorrow."

"*Au revoir!*" Mary-Kate called after her in French.

"*Adios!*" I added in Spanish.

Brittany stopped at the door and turned back to us, crossing her eyes. "Are you trying to confuse me?" she joked. Then she waved and hurried out the door.

"She's so excited about the new baby," Lauren told us. "You should see the mural she painted in the baby's room—it's beautiful! A cow and some lambs sitting in a field of daisies, with puffy clouds drifting through the sky."

Mary-Kate smiled. "Don't you think it would be fun to have a baby brother or sister?"

"Definitely," I said. "But I'm not too sure Mom would be into it. She's always saying how glad she is that we *finally* have our driver's licenses and she doesn't have to chauffeur us around anymore."

"It's too bad Brittany can't really celebrate her sweet sixteen, though," Lauren said. "We had such a good time on your birthday. I remember Brittany saying she couldn't wait to have a party of her own."

I smiled at the memory of our sweet sixteen. Mom and Dad threw us a big party at a beautiful house overlooking the ocean. The food was perfect, the music was great, all our friends were dressed up. It was one of the best nights of our lives. And to top it off, Mom and Dad gave me and Mary-Kate a pink Mustang convertible as a birthday present!

"Hey," I said, an idea brewing in my mind. "Maybe Brittany's parents are too busy to throw her a party this year—but that doesn't mean someone else can't do it!"

Mary-Kate perked up. "You mean—us?"

"Why not?" I said. "Let her parents give her the greatest seventeenth birthday party ever but sixteen is the big year!"

Lauren nodded. "And Brittany deserves a great party."

"Right," I agreed. "Let's throw her a surprise party!"

"I love it!" Mary-Kate cried. "She'll never expect it."

"Especially if we do it on Saturday—the day *after* her birthday," I added.

"We could have it right here at Click," Lauren said.

"It's perfect," I said. "She comes here all the time. We won't even have to think up an excuse to get her here!"

"Do they do private parties?" Mary-Kate asked.

"Why not?" I said. "I'll go ask Malcolm."

I went up to the counter. Malcolm glanced up from his book.

"It's important," I assured him. "We'd like to reserve a date for a private party."

Malcolm stared at me. "Here?" he asked.

"Yes," I replied. "Don't you think it would be perfect?"

"I guess," Malcolm said. "But the party had better be soon—real soon."

"Why?" I asked.

"Haven't you heard?" Malcolm said. "Click is going out of business."

chapter two

"Going out of business!" I gasped. "Why?"

"Because it doesn't make enough money, that's why," Malcolm answered.

"But my friends and I come here all the time!" I protested.

"Sure, but that's not enough," Malcolm said. "Coffee Heaven opened three new stores this year and they're all within a few miles of us. They're drawing away a lot of our customers."

"But Click is so much cooler than Coffee Heaven! It can't close!"

Malcolm shrugged. "I don't see what we can do about it."

I was shocked. How could Click go out of business? It was such a great place. And besides, we needed a place to hold Brittany's party.

"How soon are you closing?" I asked

Malcolm. "Will you still be open two weeks from Saturday?"

Malcolm glanced at a calendar. "The twenty-third? Sure, I think so. I'll have to check with Tanya." Tanya was the manager. "But it's probably fine. Leave me your phone number. I'll have Tanya call you."

"Great." I scribbled my name and number on a scrap of paper and left it with Malcolm.

This place can't *close,* I thought as I stared at the funky green walls and cushiony couches. *There's got to be a way to save it.*

"Coffee Heaven is taking over the world!" Mary-Kate groaned. "At this rate there'll be one on every block!"

"I know." I sighed. Coffee Heaven was fine, but it wasn't *our* place. Not like Click.

"At least we can have Brittany's party there," I said. "Tanya said it was no problem. She's not even charging us for use of the room."

"That's cool." Mary-Kate leaned back against the pillows on my bed and frowned.

"Hey, don't get so excited," I teased. "What's the matter?"

"I don't know." She sighed. "Don't you think Jake looked great this afternoon?"

So that was it. "Sure," I replied. "He usually does."

"Ashley, do you think I made a mistake?" she asked. "Breaking up with Jake, I mean."

I shrugged. "I understand why you did it," I told her. "You started to wonder if maybe he wasn't as nice a guy as you thought."

"Yeah," she said. "But what if I was wrong?"

"I don't know," I said. "But one thing I do know—you two are very compatible."

"How do you know that?" Mary-Kate asked.

"Mostly just by the way you guys get along together," I said. "But there's also my Theory of Compatibility."

She sat up. "Your what?"

"Theory of Compatibility," I repeated. "You and Jake score really high."

She raised an eyebrow. "*What* are you talking about?"

I pulled out my math notebook. "I figured this out in math class the other day," I said, flipping open the notebook. "See, there are two categories—Interests & Personality and Goals & Values." I showed her a graph I'd made in the notebook.

"Most people think it's important to have a lot in common," I explained. "But that's not true—look at Jennifer and Tom."

Jennifer and Tom were seniors at school. They were one of those odd couples who have nothing in common—and I mean *nothing*—but get along great. Jennifer was a vegetarian, heavily into politics and animal rights. Tom was a steak-chomping football player. Nobody could understand why they were together, but they were totally in love.

"So?" Mary-Kate said.

"So I figured out a formula," I told her. "It's not how much you have in common with a guy. It's the *ratio* of common interests to common values. The ratio of Category One to Category Two. Jennifer and Tom have zero interests in common and zero goals or values in common. Their personalities are nothing alike. Zeros across the board. So both categories are even. They're balanced." I paused. "We happened to be doing something with ratios in math class that day."

"You are seriously deranged," Mary-Kate joked.

I laughed. "Give me a chance. Let's say you have five interests in common with a guy but only one similar goal or value. The ratio would be five to one. That's not good."

Mary-Kate shook her head. "This doesn't make any sense."

I ignored her. "There's one clincher, though. If, completely independently, you and your crush have the same favorite song *and* favorite book, nothing else matters. You're made for each other! You and Jake both love *Great Expectations*, right?" I said, naming her favorite Charles Dickens novel.

She nodded.

"And before you even started going out, you both had the same favorite song!" I finished. "You have the clincher. That means you're a good couple."

Mary-Kate laughed. "You sure are into this theory of yours. You should start a matchmaking service."

"I'll get right on that," I said. "As soon as I find a way to keep Click from closing, and maybe save the world while I'm at it."

"Let's just worry about Click for now," Mary-Kate said. "Though you'd be a great matchmaker and people love stuff like that."

I could almost see the lightbulb flashing over my head.

"That's it!" I cried. "That's the perfect way to bring more customers to Click—and keep it from closing!"

"What is?" Mary-Kate looked confused.

"A matchmaking service!" I said. "I'll start one at Click. Everybody will love it!"

"And you can put your theory to the test," Mary-Kate added. "See if it really works."

"Oh, it works," I assured her. "You'll see."

"We've got only two weeks until Brittany's birthday," I said the next day. "That's not much time."

I glanced at Ashley. If there was one thing we learned from planning our own sweet sixteen, it was that the earlier you start, the better.

Lauren sipped her soda. We were eating lunch in the cafeteria and talking about Brittany's surprise party. "Why don't we meet at Click tonight?" she suggested. "We can look it over and decide how we want to set up the party and what kind of decorations we'll need."

Ashley nodded. "Good idea. Should we do a theme party or—"

I spotted Brittany across the room, beelining toward us. "Shhhh . . . Brittany's coming."

Ashley stopped talking. We were all quiet when Brittany sat down next to me.

"Hey there," she said. We grinned at her. I have to admit, it must have looked suspicious. Brittany's no fool.

"Were you just talking about me?" she asked. "You sure are quiet all of a sudden."

"No way!" Lauren said a little too loudly. "We weren't talking about you. Not at all."

"Why would we talk about you?" Ashley asked. "Is there something we should know?"

Brittany gave her a strange look. "Not that I can think of."

"Um . . . I was talking about Jake," I lied. "And he walked by, and I didn't want him to hear me—"

Brittany glanced around the room. "Where is he? I don't see him."

"He left," Ashley said. "So, what have you got for lunch there, Britt? Vegetable soup?"

"Uh-huh." Brittany blew on her soup and tasted it. She made a sour face. "I give it negative four stars."

"That's what you get for being adventurous," Lauren said.

Brittany laughed. "Yeah—if by adventurous you mean trying anything the cafeteria serves other than ice cream." She pushed her soup away. "So what's going on this weekend? I've got another surfing lesson tomorrow."

"Cool," I said. "You must be getting good. You go surfing almost every weekend."

"It's so much fun," Brittany said. "And the guys are totally hot. I don't really need to take lessons anymore, but my teacher is so cute!"

We all laughed.

"So, girls, what about tonight?" Brittany asked. "Anything happening?"

"I think I'm going to stay in tonight," Lauren said.

"Really?" Brittany said. "It's Friday! Isn't there a party or something?"

"Not that I know of," Ashley said. "We'll probably hang out at home tonight, too—right, Mary-Kate?"

I nodded. "I'm pretty beat. It's been a really long week."

"Too bad," Brittany said. "I kind of feel like doing something."

"Maybe tomorrow night," I suggested.

"What's with you guys?" Brittany gave us each a funny look. "It's Friday night and you don't want to go out?" She grabbed me by the shoulders and shook me lightly. "What have you done with my friends?"

Lauren, Ashley, and I plastered innocent grins on our faces and shrugged.

"I'm glad you stopped by, Mary-Kate," Ms. Barbour said later that afternoon. "I'll introduce you to everyone."

She welcomed me into the Website room. A few kids I recognized as seniors sat in front of computer monitors, clicking away.

"We're going to start the real work on Monday," Ms. Barbour told me. "We'll meet after school, put together an editorial plan, and assign jobs to the editors. How does that sound?"

"Great!" I said, glancing around the room. The walls were plastered with posters and color photocopies of movie stills, fashion photos, interesting graphics—all kinds of cool images. I could tell this Website was going to be something really new and fun, not just another version of the school paper.

Ms. Barbour led me to a desk where a skinny girl sat surfing the Web. The girl glanced up at me and smiled. She was pretty, with brown hair cut into a neat chin-length bob and a fringe of bangs over wide dark eyes.

"Do you know Stacy Segal?" Ms. Barbour asked. I shook my head. Stacy was a senior. I'd seen her around over the years, but we'd never met. "She's going to be the editor in chief of the Website, so you'll be working under her. She'll give you assignments and help you with any problems that come up. Stacy, this is Mary-Kate Olsen."

"Hi." Stacy nodded at me.

I smiled at her. "Hi."

"Mary-Kate is a talented photographer," Ms. Barbour told Stacy. "I think she'll make a good photo editor. But we can discuss all that on Monday."

Ms. Barbour excused herself and went off to talk to another student. I glanced at the monitor in front of Stacy.

"I'm checking out all the teen Websites," Stacy explained to me, "looking for new ideas to suggest at the meeting on Monday."

"Did you ever check out this site?" I asked, typing a Website address into the computer. "They update it every day with fashion tips and stuff like that. I log on to it every morning before school starts."

Stacy grinned as the site came up. "So do I! I was thinking we could do something like that on our school site—you know, a tip for the day, something fun that's going on."

"Great idea," I agreed.

"I'm so psyched to be working with Ms. Barbour," Stacy said in a low voice. "I mean, she used to work at *Fashion Daily*! I'm trying to get into the journalism program at UCLA next year. And if I can get a good recommendation from her, I'm in for sure."

"She's very businesslike," I said. "But she seems nice."

"She obviously likes your photos a lot," Stacy said. "She told me she wanted the most talented kids in school on the staff. Your stuff must be amazing!"

I didn't know what to say, so I just smiled. Stacy made the Website sound like a special club—Ms. Barbour's chosen few. I hoped I could live up to it.

❀

"A matchmaking service?" Tanya, the manager of Click, blinked her big gray eyes at me. It was Friday evening and I was waiting for Lauren and Mary-Kate to show up.

Tanya wore her bleached blond hair in tiny little pigtails all over her head. "I never thought of that, Ashley. How would it work?"

"I'll make up a questionnaire for people to fill out," I explained. "They can list their likes and dislikes, what they're looking for, anything they want to say about themselves. And I'll take a picture of each person." I'd figured it all out last night. I couldn't wait to get started!

"We'll put everything in a notebook. Kids can come into the café, flip through the book, and see if there's anybody they want to ask out. Even if they're not looking for dates, it would be fun just to check out the photos and read what people wrote about themselves."

"I love it!" Tanya cried. "That could really bring in a lot of kids."

Malcolm glanced up from the magazine he was reading—*The Journal of Pediatric Medicine*. "You've got to be kidding me, Tanya," he said. "You're not really going to do this, are you? Will I have to stand here behind this counter and watch a bunch of high school kids checking each other out?"

I made a face at Malcolm. High school kids! He was a junior at Bayside himself!

"Sorry, Malcolm," Tanya said. "It might be the only way to save Click. You don't want to lose this job, do you?"

Malcolm shrugged. "It wouldn't exactly break my heart."

"Here's the best part," I told Tanya. "I invented a formula for finding the perfect match. If they want to, people can apply my formula to their potential dates and see who they're compatible with."

"That sounds like fun," Tanya said. "All right, Ashley. You are now the official house matchmaker of Click Café!"

"Excellent!" I was very excited. I just knew that people would love my dating service—and Click would stay open for business.

I sat at a table and opened my sparkly purple notebook. I'd started jotting down ideas for the dating questionnaire when Lauren and Mary-Kate walked in and sat down with me.

"So, how did Tanya like your idea?" Mary-Kate asked.

I showed her what I'd written in my notebook. DO YOU CLICK? TWENTY QUESTIONS FOR CLICK DATING FORM: 1—NAME, 2—AGE, 3—

"It's a go!" I announced.

"Yes!" Lauren cheered.

"You can advertise it on the new school Website," Mary-Kate offered.

"Perfect." I jotted it down. "And the school paper, too." Then I turned to another section of my notebook and wrote: BRITTANY'S SURPRISE PARTY.

"All right," I said. "What kind of decorations do we want for Brittany's party?"

"How about a big poster of Brittany?" Mary-Kate suggested. "I could blow up one of her baby pictures and put it next to a recent photo of her. You know, Brittany now and Brittany then."

"Great idea," I said, writing in my notebook.

"She's really into surfing lately," Lauren said. "We could do kind of a Hawaiian luau theme, lots of flowers, leis, tropical punch—"

"—and surfer music!" Mary-Kate added.

I scribbled all this down. "This party is going to totally rock," I said. "What else can we do?"

I looked up from my notebook and happened to glance through the window of the café.

"Oh, no!" I whispered. "It's Brittany! And she sees us!"

Lauren and Mary-Kate turned around before I could stop them. Brittany was staring at us, looking hurt.

"She's coming in!" Lauren said. "What are we going to do?"

chapter three

"Don't panic," Ashley whispered, slamming her notebook shut. "Act normal! Wave to her!"

"But we all told her we weren't doing anything tonight," Lauren said through her teeth. "And now she catches us all out together. What are we going to say?"

"We'll think of something." I smiled and waved Brittany over to our table.

"Hey," Brittany said, looking warily at the three of us. "What are you guys doing here?"

I glanced at Ashley. "Ashley and I came to pitch her idea to Tanya. You know, about the dating service? Tanya loves it!"

"That's good," Brittany said, her eyes moving to Lauren.

"And we just happened to run into Lauren!" Ashley added.

"But why didn't you call me?" Brittany asked Lauren. "You knew I wanted to do something tonight. Normally you'd call me if you were going to Click or somewhere."

"Of course I would," Lauren said. "But I wasn't planning on coming here. My—um—my mother sent me out to do an errand for her. I saw Mary-Kate and Ashley walk in here so I stopped in to see them."

Brittany pulled up a chair and sat down. That was a good sign. Her face relaxed. She seemed to be buying our lame stories.

"So what do you have to do for your mom?" Brittany asked Lauren.

A flicker of panic flashed over Lauren's face. "She's sick," Lauren lied. "She needed me to pick up a prescription at the pharmacy."

Brittany looked concerned. "What's wrong with her?" she asked.

Lauren glanced desperately around the room, searching for something to tell Brittany. I cringed. This wasn't going too well.

I followed Lauren's eyes toward Malcolm and his *Journal of Pediatric Medicine*. One of the headlines on the cover read "Pediculosis—a new solution?"

"Pediculosis!" Lauren said. "Mom's got a bad case of pediculosis."

Whatever that is, I thought.

Brittany nodded. "That sounds awful! I'm sorry to hear that."

"She'll be okay," Lauren said. "She just needs a little rest—and some medicine."

Ashley opened her notebook to her dating service section. I knew she was trying to change the subject. "Come on, you guys. Help me think up questions for my matchmaking form."

Brittany perked up. "You could have fill-in-the-blanks," she suggested. "Like, 'People always say I'm too "blank."'"

Good move, Ashley, I thought. The old change-the-subject trick. Brittany had already stopped wondering what we were all doing without her.

That was a close one.

CLICK CAFÉ DATING QUESTIONNAIRE: DO YOU CLICK?

Section One: Who I Am

Name: ______________________________

Age: ______________________________

Grade: ______________________________

School: ______________________________

E-mail Address: ______________________________

Do you want Ashley to suggest a match for you using her Theory of Compatibility? (circle one) Yes No

Hobbies and Interests: ______________________________

____

Favorite Things:

Book: ______________ Movie: ______________

Band: ____________ Song: ____________
Color: ____________ Food: ____________
School Subject: ____________ Teacher: ____________
Artist: ____________ Actor: ____________
Actress: ____________ TV Show: ____________
Animal: ____________ Historical Period: ____________
Way to waste time: ____________
Five things I can't live without: 1.________ 2.________
3.________ 4.________ 5.________
The most outrageous lie I've ever told:

My most embarrassing moment:

The most important thing to know about me is:

Why you should get to know me:

Section Two: Who I Want to Be and Stuff that Matters to Me

Fill in the blanks:
My friends say I'm too ____________
My friends say they like the way I ____________
I hate it when my date ____________
I like it when my date ____________
I'm looking for someone who ____________

I'm interested in only dating people who have (circle as many as apply and add more if you like):
Good looks A good heart

Brains	A love of animals
Sense of humor	A dislike of animals
Good grades	A good appetite
Nice clothes	A cool car
Other: ____________	

I won't date someone who:
Dyes their hair
Eats meat
Doesn't eat meat
Wears a nose ring
Other: ____________

These things are important to me:

My goals for this year are:

My goals for the next five years are:

My goals for life are:

"You just fill out this questionnaire," I said, handing a form to a giggly girl with braces. I was spending Sunday afternoon at Click, setting up the dating service. Word had traveled fast, and Click was already buzzing with new customers.

"When you're finished," I told the girl, "I'll take your picture and put you in the book. Or you can look through the book and see if there are any boys you want to ask out."

"Thanks, Ashley." The girl giggled again and took the form to a table. For the first time since I'd been coming to Click, most of the tables were full—and on a Sunday! I smiled at Tanya, who was busy helping Malcolm behind the counter. *I've done it!* I thought. *I saved Click!*

Kids were busy filling out questionnaires and lining up to have their picture taken. I even spotted Aaron Moore at the big table in the corner. Of course, five girls sat around him, filling out questionnaires and reading their answers to him.

He's the last person on earth who needs a dating service, I thought as I watched him. Aaron was tall and athletic with dark wavy hair just a little too long. Something about the way it flopped over his dark blue eyes made it hard to stop staring at him.

Snap out of it, Ashley, I told myself. I'd never even thought of dating Aaron—not seriously, at least. He was totally cute and the coolest guy in my whole class, but he was always surrounded by girls. Still, it was a good sign that he was hanging out here at Click—it meant that the café was becoming *the* place to be.

Someone dropped a filled-out questionnaire on my table. "I'm ready for my picture now, Ashley," a girl announced. I was surprised to see Sarah Hunter, a pretty, olive-skinned girl with long, frizzy auburn hair and hazel eyes.

"*You're* looking for a date?" I asked Sarah.

"But what about Warren?" Sarah had been dating Warren Voigt since the ninth grade. In everybody's minds they were a unit—SarahandWarren.

"We broke up," Sarah explained. She said it kind of crisply, like it was none of my business. Maybe she was getting sick of people being so surprised about it. "Your matchmaking service is just what I need to help me get over him."

I shrugged. "Okay. Stand against this wall and I'll take your picture."

The questionnaires poured in all afternoon. Soon I had enough to fill two notebooks—one for boys and one for girls. I glanced at the answers as I filed them, especially those on the boys' forms. In the back of my mind I was keeping an eye out for a good match for Mary-Kate. I knew Mary-Kate missed Jake. Maybe a new guy was just what she needed to take her mind off him.

I took the notebooks home with me that night. After dinner I sat on my bed for hours, poring over the questionnaires. I saw a few that looked promising for Mary-Kate, but there was always some little problem—like the guy whose goal was world domination.

Then I found it. When I first looked over the questionnaire, I didn't think too much of it. But I applied my Theory of Compatibility to it anyway. I crunched the numbers. And they worked!

Yes! I cheered. I found a winner for Mary-Kate!

chapter four

"I want this Website to be the talk of the school," Ms. Barbour said. It was Monday afternoon, and the first meeting of the new school Website was just coming to an end. I sat beside Stacy, whose eyes were shining as she hung on Ms. Barbour's every word.

"The Bayside High Website will be completely different from the school paper," Ms. Barbour continued. "It will be the *anti*-paper. No reports from the school senate meetings. No editorials about how we need soda machines in the student lounge. We want to cover what the students are *really* interested in. Any questions?"

I raised my hand. "Yes, Mary-Kate?" Ms. Barbour said.

"When will the Website be up?" I asked.

"I hope to have it ready in two weeks," Ms.

Barbour replied. "And we'll update it as often as possible—every day if we can. Anything else?"

No one said anything. "All right," Ms. Barbour finished. "You've got your assignments. I'm here if you need any help. See you all tomorrow."

"Don't you love her, Mary-Kate?" Stacy asked as we filed out of the Website office. "She makes me feel so professional."

I nodded. "I like our first assignment. Want to start working on it now? I'll stop by my locker and get my camera."

Stacy and I had been assigned to do a fashion piece on school trends, starting with the boys. Stacy was going to write the story and I would take the photos.

"Baseball practice is almost over," Stacy said. "Let's wait outside the gym and catch the guys as they leave."

We stationed ourselves on the gym steps. A few minutes later, the boys from the baseball team began to file out.

"There's Aaron Moore," Stacy whispered. "Let's interview him. He always looks good."

We approached Aaron, who was talking to Erik Douglas, one of his teammates. "Hey, guys," Stacy said. "Can we talk to you for a second?"

"Sure," Aaron said. He was wearing jeans, sneakers, and a red T-shirt with the name of a seventies rock band printed on it. Nothing special, but it looked good on him. Erik was kind of burly, pumped up from too much weight lifting, and his khaki shorts didn't fit him as well.

"We're working on the new school Website," I explained, focusing my camera on them. "Can we take your picture and ask you a few questions about your style?"

Aaron smiled shyly. "Style? I have a style?"

Erik grinned and put on a corny, pumping-iron pose. "Maybe *you* don't, Moore, but these girls know style when they see it. Am I right, girls?"

I laughed and snapped pictures of both of them. Stacy interviewed them about what kinds of clothes they liked and which celebrities they wanted to look like.

Three more boys burst out of the gym. I aimed my camera at one, waiting for him to get a little closer. *He looks good,* I thought, noticing his corduroys and blue button-down shirt. Then I saw his face. It was Jake. Without thinking, I snapped his picture.

"Thanks, guys," Stacy said to Aaron and Erik. "Let's talk to these three now," she said to me, nodding at Jake and his two friends.

I took a deep breath. I wasn't sure I *could* talk to him. So I stood off to the side and photographed the boys while Stacy interviewed them. Jake smiled and nodded at me. But he didn't try to talk to me or anything.

"I never realized how many cute guys go to this school," Stacy gushed as Jake and his friends walked away. "Our assignment forces us to notice them!"

I laughed, but I didn't need a reason to notice Jake.

"What did Jake say when you saw him?" Ashley asked me at dinner that night. Mom and Dad had gone out to eat, so Ashley and I ordered in sushi. I plucked a piece of tuna with my chopsticks and dipped it in soy sauce.

"Nothing," I told her. "It was kind of awkward."

"Well, forget about him," Ashley said. "For now, anyway. I've got some news that will take your mind off him."

"What is it?" I asked.

"You've got a date!" she announced.

The tuna slipped out of my chopsticks and plopped onto my plate. "What? What are you talking about?"

"I was looking through some of my Click dating questionnaires and I happened to find the perfect guy for you," she explained. "No need to thank me. It's just part of my job."

I frowned. "I do miss Jake," I admitted. "That's true. But I don't really feel like dating right now. I've got enough going on with school and the Website. . . ."

"Mary-Kate, you have to try it," Ashley insisted. "For the good of Click Café. How will it look if my own sister won't use my matchmaking service? Please?"

I sighed. "All right—but just once. Who's this dream guy you've picked out for me?"

Ashley grinned. "I applied my theory to him and you, and the score wasn't perfect, but it was pretty close."

"Who is it?" I asked again.

"Mike Mott," Ashley said.

My jaw dropped open. How could Ashley do this to me? "Mike Mott!" I protested. "That dorky skater dude? Come on, Ashley. Mike Mott and I have nothing in common. Zero!"

"That's not true," Ashley insisted. "You'd be surprised how much you can find out about people from these questionnaires. Turns out you and Mike Mott have the same favorite color—blue; the same favorite animal—dogs; and the same favorite teacher—Mr. Burkett!"

I rolled my eyes. "Big deal. Everybody likes dogs, the color blue, and Mr. Burkett."

"Yeah, but not everybody says they can't live without lip balm," Ashley said. "But you can't—and neither can Mike Mott."

"Mike Mott uses lip balm?" I had trouble

believing it. Lip balm obsession was such a girly thing.

Ashley nodded. "He wears SPF 45. I guess because he's outside in the sun on his skateboard all the time."

"I still don't think it's much to go on," I insisted.

"According to my theory, you two should get along," Ashley said. "Come on, Mary-Kate. Just go out with him once and see. What can it hurt?"

"All right," I agreed with a sigh. "But I'm doing it only to help you and the café."

"Thanks, Mary-Kate." Ashley stood up and threw her arms around my neck. "You won't be sorry."

I thought of Mike Mott, with his baggy skater's shorts, hair dyed blond in front, and his weird skater lingo, and shuddered. "I hope you're right. But I doubt it."

❀

"I had a brainstorm last night," Lauren told me. "You are going to love this, Ashley." We were sitting at Click after school the next day. "You know when you wake up and a great idea hits you like a bolt of lightning?"

I nodded. "Yeah, that happens to me every day," I joked.

"Okay—I thought of the perfect present for Brittany's birthday," Lauren said. "A customized surfboard!"

"You're a genius!" I cried. It was a great idea. Brittany loved surfing, but she didn't have her own board. "We can all chip in and get a really great one—yellow, with her name on it, and maybe a butterfly." Yellow was Brittany's favorite color, and she loved butterflies.

"My brother told me about a place in Huntington Beach where they sell custom boards," Lauren said. "You and Mary-Kate and I could drive down there and get it."

"Road trip! I love it!" I exclaimed.

"I knew you would," Lauren said, pulling a catalog from her backpack and passing it to me. "I'll call the shop and order it as soon as I get home. Brittany's party is less than two weeks away, and I think you have to order custom boards at least ten days ahead of time."

I flipped through the catalog. It was full of all kinds of surfer gear.

"I've got some more lonelyhearts here for you," Tanya said. She dropped a pile of questionnaires and photos on my table. She took photos of the applicants when I wasn't around.

"Thanks, Tanya," I said. I gave the catalog back to Lauren. "I'd better start going through these," I told her, thumbing through the papers. "They pile up fast."

Lauren picked up a questionnaire and skimmed it. "These are so funny," she said. "Listen to this—'Five things I can't live without: Beef patties, buns, pickles, ketchup, and onions.' Why didn't he just say hamburgers?"

"Here's one with no photo," I said, picking up a form. The first thing I saw was "Name—Mysterio." Mysterio was a superhero in a popular comic book series. He was a handsome teenager with the power to turn invisible.

This must be a joke, I thought. I skimmed over the form. At the bottom was a note.

To Ashley—This is not a joke. I need to be anonymous, for my own reasons. But I want to test your Theory of Compatibility. I'm curious—who will you fix me up with? Send your possible matches to my school E-mail address. If I'm interested in dating the girl you suggest, I will reveal my identity and call her.

I still thought it had to be a joke. Somebody at school was teasing me. But as I read the rest of the questionnaire, I started to wonder. Maybe it wasn't a joke after all.

Whoever filled out the form was very sweet and thoughtful. His favorite way to waste time was lying in the grass, staring at clouds. The one thing he was looking for in a girl was a good heart. Under "Why you should get to know me" he wrote, "Because the real me is different from the person everybody thinks they know—but nobody at school really knows me. Nobody has ever tried to find the real me. I hope I can find a girl who wants to know what I'm really like behind my mask."

I was very curious. Who was Mysterio?

chapter five

"These photos are wonderful, Mary-Kate," Ms. Barbour said the next afternoon. She scanned the pictures I'd taken of boys and their fashion choices.

"Let's use these three to illustrate Stacy's article." She pointed at pictures of Jake, Aaron, and another boy. "Give me some captions for them by the end of the day. I'll have a new assignment for you tomorrow."

"Okay," I said. She disappeared into her small office and closed the door. I sat at a desk and got to work. I stared at the three photos and tried to think of something clever to write.

Stacy came in and settled in front of a computer. "What are you doing?" she asked me.

"Writing captions," I told her.

She popped a disk into a drive and pressed a

key. "I'll look them over before you show them to Ms. Barbour if you want," she offered.

"Thanks," I said. "That would be great." Stacy had more experience with this kind of thing than I did.

An hour later, I showed Stacy the captions I'd written. "These are really good," she told me. "Maybe I'd shorten this one a little bit." She crossed out a few words. As soon as she did it, I realized she was right—the sentence was a little too long.

"Thanks," I said. I knocked on Ms. Barbour's office door and gave her the captions. She read them over quickly. "Good work, Mary-Kate!" she said. "You have a real flair with words. Have you ever thought of going into the magazine business after college? I think you'd have a real talent for it."

"Thank you." My cheeks flushed at the compliment. Ms. Barbour thought I was talented!

I went back to my desk to get my backpack. Stacy flashed me a thumbs-up.

"Way to go!" she whispered. She must have overheard what Ms. Barbour had said to me. "When someone like Ms. Barbour says you're talented, she's not kidding. You've got it made!"

"Thanks," I said. I didn't want to make a big deal out of it, but I felt my face glowing.

"Oh, Mary-Kate." Ms. Barbour came out of her office. "I'm having some very large posters designed to advertise the new Website. I want everyone in school to be aware of it."

"That's a great idea!" Stacy said.

"Thank you," Ms. Barbour said. "The ads *must* be at the printer by tomorrow afternoon if they're going to be ready in time for our launch. I can't take them myself because I've got a very important appointment. I'd like you to drop them off at the printer after school tomorrow."

"Sure," I agreed.

"I'll leave the address and the ads on my desk," Ms. Barbour said. "They'll be in a large envelope."

"No problem," I said. "I'll make sure they get to the printer."

"Thanks, Mary-Kate," Ms. Barbour said. "I'm counting on you."

❀

"Check this out," I said to Mary-Kate when she came into Click Tuesday night. I flipped open the surfer catalog. I was swamped with matchmaking requests and had already spent hours that day applying my theory to stacks of questionnaires.

"Here it is," I said, folding back the page in the catalog and passing it to Mary-Kate. "We're going to get Brittany this surfboard for her birthday—customized!"

"It's beautiful," Mary-Kate said. "She'll love it!"

"Lauren already ordered it," I told her. "But it won't be ready until the day before Brittany's party. We had to put a rush on it as it was."

Mary-Kate glanced at the address on the catalog. "But this place is all the way down in Huntington Beach," she said. "That's at least an hour's drive away. Do they deliver?"

I shook my head. "We'll have to drive down and pick up the board after school next Friday." I took the catalog from her and stuffed it into my backpack. "We've got to hide the catalog. Brittany and Lauren are meeting us here any minute."

"Let me just show you this before they get here," Mary-Kate said. She pulled a piece of paper out of her bag. "Here's what the party invitations will look like. I'm going to print them out tonight."

The card showed one of Mary-Kate's photos of Brittany—a really pretty shot. I grinned. "It's perfect," I said. "This is going to be the best surprise!"

She snatched the card away from me and hid it in her bag. "Quick—here they come!"

"Hey, guys," Lauren said. She and Brittany settled at our table. "What's up?"

"Take a look at this," I said, passing Mysterio's questionnaire to Brittany. Mary-Kate and Lauren read it over her shoulder.

"'Mysterio,'" Brittany read. "Who is it?"

"That's what I'd like to know," I said. "Any guesses?"

"I have no clue," Mary-Kate said.

"He seems like kind of a nice guy," Brittany commented, reading on. "If this is for real," she added.

"Maybe it's a girl," Lauren guessed.

"But why would a girl do something like this?" I asked.

Lauren shrugged. "On second thought, I guess she probably wouldn't."

"Here you go," Malcolm said. He stopped at our table and set down two tall iced coffees. "Two Mystery Specials."

"Who do you think Mysterio is?" I asked him. He'd been watching me puzzle over the mystery all evening.

"A loser," Malcolm snapped. "This whole dating service thing is so bogus."

I frowned. "When's the last time *you* went on a date, Malcolm?" I asked.

"None of your business," he replied, slinking back behind the counter. He picked up his magazine, *Conspiracy Theorist's Digest*, and hid behind it.

"I'll bet he hasn't been out with a girl in a year," Mary-Kate said.

"I'll bet he's *never* been on a date," Brittany added. "Who'd go out with him? He sneers at everything."

"Hey," I said. "Maybe that's the answer."

"What are you talking about?" Mary-Kate asked.

"Malcolm!" I said. "Maybe he's Mysterio! Maybe he's playing a joke on me. He thinks the match-making service is silly."

"Yeah," Lauren added. "But maybe deep down he's secretly hoping he gets a date out of it!"

It was starting to make sense. "This could be his weird, roundabout way of asking for my help!" I whispered.

"I don't know," Mary-Kate said, reading over Mysterio's questionnaire. "I mean, could Malcolm really write something like this? 'My goals in life are to find out what I'm meant to do, do it well, and share it with someone who loves me'?"

"I don't know," I admitted. "But I'm about to find out."

I stood up and marched over to the counter. Malcolm put down his magazine. "What's wrong, not enough mocha in your latte?"

"You're Mysterio, aren't you," I said. "You're playing a joke on me, right?"

Malcolm stared at me in shock for a second. Then he burst out laughing.

"Me? You think *I'm* your mystery dude?" He choked with laughter. "That's great! You really think I'd go to the trouble of filling out a fake form just to play a lame joke on you?"

He laid his head down on *Conspiracy Theorist's Digest* and practically sobbed with laughter. "You crack me up, Ashley," he said. "You really do."

I glanced back at the others. Mary-Kate shook her head. I sighed and walked back to the table.

"I guess I was wrong," I said.

Mary-Kate patted me on the arm. "It really doesn't look like he's your man."

"I'm glad it's not him," Lauren said. "I don't want this to turn out to be a joke. I want Mysterio to be real! There's something so romantic about him."

Inside, I agreed with Lauren. I wanted Mysterio to be real, too.

"All right, then," I said. "Who should we fix him up with?"

"Let me see some of these questionnaires." Brittany grabbed a stack of forms and started riffling through them. "What about this girl?" she suggested, holding up a form filled out in loopy handwriting and pink ink. "Ali Riggs. She's looking for someone who has a good heart, just like Mysterio. And they both like feta cheese omelets!"

I scanned Ali's questionnaire. She was a cute girl. Lots of guys had crushes on her. Why not?

"Good," I said. "I'll talk to Ali at school tomorrow and see if she'll do it. It might not be easy to talk her into it. I mean, I can't tell her who I'm fixing her up with."

"Just ask her," Mary-Kate said. "If she says okay, you can E-mail Mysterio. Then maybe he'll reveal his identity!"

"Yeah," Brittany added. "I don't really care whether Ali and Mysterio get together—but I'm dying to find out who this guy is."

"That reminds me," I said to Mary-Kate. "You're free this Saturday night, right?"

She nodded. "Why?"

"Good," I said. "Your date with Mike Mott is all set. I talked to him this afternoon. He's looking forward to it."

Mary-Kate sighed. "Well, I'm not. I'm not really in the mood for dating right now."

Brittany laughed. "Mike Mott? You're fixing Mary-Kate up with *him*?"

"I told you he's not right for me, Ashley," Mary-Kate said.

"You should be more open-minded," I scolded them. "Both of you. We hardly know Mike. How can you be so sure he's not right for Mary-Kate? He was very friendly when I talked to him today."

"But he's one of those skater guys," Brittany said. "He does nothing but skateboard every chance he gets! He rides his board between classes. He probably sleeps with it!"

"And I'm not a skater," Mary-Kate reminded me, as if I didn't know.

"That can't be *all* he does," I objected. "Nobody is that simple."

"We'll see," Brittany said.

"Yeah," Mary-Kate added. "I guess I'll find out Saturday night what Mike Mott's other interests are—if any."

Over her shoulder, the café door opened and Jake walked in. *Uh-oh,* I thought. *I hope Mary-Kate doesn't spot him.* Lately she seemed to get kind of down whenever she ran into him.

He sat down on a couch and picked up one of my notebooks filled with dating questionnaires. He started flipping through it.

Oh, no! What's he doing?

Mary-Kate noticed me watching him. "Who are you looking at?" she asked. She turned around and saw him.

"He's looking through one of your dating books!" Lauren whispered. "Does that mean—"

Mary-Kate nodded sadly. "He must be looking for a new girlfriend!"

chapter six

Jake glanced up. I quickly turned around to face Ashley.

"Did he see me looking?" I asked.

Ashley shook her head. "I don't think so."

My heart sank. I couldn't believe it. Jake and I had broken up only a few weeks ago. And he was already looking for someone else!

I was still mad at him, but I missed him, too. How could he get over me so easily? How could he be looking for a new girlfriend so soon?

"Maybe you're right, Ashley," I said. "Maybe I *should* try dating someone else."

"All right!" Ashley cheered. "That's the spirit! You'll have a good time on Saturday night, you'll see."

I glanced back toward Jake. He was intently reading a questionnaire.

I hoped Ashley was right.

"And don't worry," Ashley whispered to me. "It's going to be very hard for me to find a good match for Jake—if you know what I mean."

Lauren and Brittany giggled. I grinned. Maybe having the matchmaker-in-chief for a sister wasn't so bad after all.

The Website office was empty when I went in after school the next day. I stepped into Ms. Barbour's little office within the office and flicked on the light. There was a package on her desk with a Post-it that had my name on it. Beside the package was a scrap of paper.

This must be the printer's address, I thought, picking up the paper and the package. I turned out the lights and hurried out to my car.

A bunch of guys were doing skateboard tricks in the school parking lot. "Hey, Mike, look who it is," one boy called when he saw me.

I glanced across the lot. Mike Mott screeched to a stop on his board, then slowly rolled toward me. He had a small, wiry build—he still kind of looked like a little kid. A tough little kid.

"Hey, Mary-Kate," he said, kicking his board to a stop. "So—Saturday night, huh?"

"Yeah. Saturday night." My stomach tightened. The more I saw of Mike, the more I dreaded Saturday night.

A couple of Mike's friends skated toward us. "Whoa," one of them teased. "Check it out."

"Mike's got a girlfriend!" another one taunted. They started making kissing noises.

"Don't pay any attention to them," Mike said. "They're idiots."

No kidding, I thought. "Well, I've got to go," I said. I headed for the Mustang, keys ready in my hand.

"Okay—see you!" Mike called after me. I started the car and drove off.

He seems like a nice enough guy, I thought, my stomach still churning with dread. *But kind of immature.*

I knew Ashley was right. I should keep my mind open—and keep Jake out of it. Still, was the fact that Mike and I both wear lip balm really enough to base a date on?

I turned right and headed downtown, glancing at the address: 1542 Loma Vista. I spotted a strip mall up ahead. *That must be it,* I thought.

I pulled into the parking lot and got out of the car, taking the package with me. There it was—1542 Loma Vista. But it wasn't a printing shop. It was a travel agency!

I stared down at the paper, double-checking the address—1542 Loma Vista. I definitely had the right place. I walked up and down the mall, searching for a printer. There wasn't one.

The address must be wrong, I thought. I pulled my cell phone out of my purse and called the school. Maybe there was someone there who could help me.

The school operator connected me with the Website office, but there was no answer.

I got back in the car and drove all over the neighborhood, searching for a printer—any printer! But I couldn't find one anywhere.

I stared at the package with the posters in it. Ms. Barbour said they had to get to the printer's today, or they wouldn't be ready in time for the Website launch. What was I going to do?

What *could* I do? I drove back to school. I knew no one would be there at this hour. But I had to try. Maybe Ms. Barbour stopped in after her appointment. Maybe Stacy or someone else would be there and know the address of the printer.

Someone had to be there, I thought, drumming my hands on the steering wheel as I waited for the light to change. Because if no one was there, the posters wouldn't be printed in time—and it would be all my fault!

chapter seven

"Who is he?" Ali asked me. I caught her in the hall between classes and showed her Mysterio's dating questionnaire.

"That's the problem," I admitted. "I have no idea. I know he goes to this school, and that's about it. So you'd be taking your chances."

"But he said he'll tell you who he is before he goes out with me, right?" Ali asked.

I nodded. "So I guess you could back out of the date if you wanted to. I mean, if he turns out to be a supercreep."

She scanned the questionnaire again and said, "Okay, why not? I'll give the guy a chance."

"Great!" I exclaimed. "I'll E-mail him today and tell him I've matched him with you. I can't wait to find out who he is!"

"Me, too," Ali said. "Let me know as soon as you find out!"

"I will," I promised. The bell rang, and Ali hurried to her next class. I had a free period, so I went to the library to E-mail Mysterio. I wrote:

To Mysterio,

I have come up with a match for you. I think you'll like her. Her name is Ali Riggs, and she's a junior. You can read more about her in the matchmaker notebook at Click. Please let me know as soon as possible if you accept this match. Thank you.—Ashley Olsen

I sent the E-mail. I knew I couldn't expect a reply right away. But my curiosity about Mysterio was driving me crazy. I decided to do a little detective work.

I headed for the principal's office. Mrs. Walsh, the school secretary, was a favorite of the students. For one thing, she looked like everybody's dream of a grandmother—soft gray hair, a little plump, with kind eyes, and a warm smile. Plus she kept a big jar of jelly beans on her desk.

"Hi, Mrs. Walsh," I said, dipping into the jelly bean jar.

"Well, look who it is," Mrs. Walsh said. "The Matchmaker of Bayside High!"

I was surprised she'd heard about it so quickly. "Yeah, well, I'm just trying to keep everybody happy," I said.

"You know, I always thought *I'd* be good at matching up the kids in this school," Mrs. Walsh said. "I know more about most of you than you'd probably like to think."

That was just what I wanted to hear. Mrs. Walsh knew everything about everybody—maybe even the secret identity of a certain mystery boy.

"I've got an especially tough case right now," I told her. "I was wondering if you could help me. I need to find out who a certain E-mail address belongs to."

"Most kids just use their names," Mrs. Walsh said. "Beyond that I can't help you, Ashley. It's confidential."

I sighed and popped a jelly bean into my mouth. "Please, Mrs. Walsh. It's really important that I find out who this is. It's the only way I can help him!"

She shook her head. "You know I can't give you information like that, Ashley. If this boy doesn't want you to know who he is, that's his business, and you should respect it."

"But how can I tell who to match him up with if I don't know who he is?" I complained.

The bell rang for the next class. "You'd better get off to class," Mrs. Walsh said. "Take a few more jelly beans for the road."

"Thanks." I dipped my hand into the jar and headed for art class.

Mr. Trask, the art teacher, was handing out large sheets of paper. "Continuing our study of portraits," he said, "last week you drew a portrait of someone sitting in front of you—me."

We laughed as he waved his hand at the wall full of misshapen drawings of his head. Some were better than others—and some were just weird.

"Now I'd like you to try to draw a portrait of someone whose image you know by heart," Mr. Trask said. "This way you can't fixate on your subject's features so much. If we're lucky, his or her personality will shine through your portrait."

I decided to draw a portrait of my mother. I drew her the way she looked when she was getting ready to go out at night. Mary-Kate and I had always loved watching her dress up.

After about forty-five minutes I looked up from my paper. I was almost finished. I glanced at the other kids' drawings. Aaron Moore was sketching a little boy who looked a lot like him—probably his younger brother. The three girls in front of me were drawing portraits of Aaron!

Oh, brother, I thought. I could see why they liked him—he was very cute. But did they have to be so obvious about it?

I stood up and walked to the back of the room to get another pencil. Bart Weinberg sat in the corner, furiously sketching. He was a small, skinny boy with glasses and a brown crew cut. Not the kind of guy you really notice much. But something caught my eye—a sticker on his notebook. I moved a little closer.

Mysterio! The sticker showed a shadowy action figure over the Mysterio comic book logo.

Aha! I thought. *I have solved the mystery! Bart Weinberg must be Mysterio!*

He's very shy, too, I told myself. So it makes perfect sense. Of course he wouldn't want girls to know his identity—he was afraid of getting rejected. Most people thought he was kind of a geek—someone who was heavily into science fiction and spent his weekends going to *Star Trek* conventions.

I leaned close to Bart and whispered, "I just sent you an E-mail, Mysterio."

His head shot up and he stared at me, startled. "What?" he asked.

"I said, I just sent you an E-mail," I repeated.

He looked a little alarmed. "Why would you do that?" Without waiting for my answer, he buried his head in his notebook again. I noticed he was drawing a portrait of Darth Vader. He clearly wanted to be left alone.

Hmmm, I thought as I made my way back to my desk. *He's playing it cooler than I thought he would.*

• • •

I checked my E-mail between every class. No message from Mysterio. Finally, at the end of the day, I checked it one last time before going home.

Yes! Mysterio had written back!

I opened the message.

Ashley—thanks for matching me with Ali. She's a very nice girl. But I don't think she's right for me. Don't ask me how I know—I just know.

Will you please try again? There must be someone out there who's right for me. Let's give your theory another chance. —Mysterio

"What?" I nearly screamed. "He's turning down a date with Ali?"

Ali Riggs was a very popular girl. All the guys would have loved to go out with her.

Bart Weinberg was not very popular. Most girls I knew were not interested in him.

So how could someone like Bart turn down someone like Ali?

Something was seriously wrong.

"Hey, Mary-Kate," Stacy said as I walked into the Website office. I glanced toward Ms. Barbour's office. Was she here? Was I in trouble?

I'd left the posters on Ms. Barbour's desk the day before with a note explaining what happened.

But I had a sinking feeling that Ms. Barbour would be upset.

"Ms. Barbour stepped out for a minute," Stacy told me, following my gaze. "She sure is in a terrible mood today."

A pang shot through my stomach. *Uh-oh.*

I tried to keep myself busy at my desk, choosing typefaces for a sports feature we were planning. But I couldn't help looking up every time the door opened.

Then Ms. Barbour walked in. "Mary-Kate, may I see you in my office, please?" she said. She stalked into her office without waiting to see if I'd follow.

I glanced at Stacy. She looked nervous for me.

I took a deep breath and went in.

chapter eight

I called the printer to check on the posters last night," Ms. Barbour said. "They told me you never showed up."

"I tried to find them," I explained. "I left you a note—"

"I *saw* the note," she snapped. "But I still don't understand. I left clear instructions for you. Did you even *try* to find the printer?"

"Yes!" I cried. "I drove all over Loma Vista. There was no printer there!"

"Loma Vista?" she said. "The printer is on Ocean Drive. I left the address right here for you, clearly printed—"

"Ocean Drive?" I was amazed. "But the address was 1542 Loma Vista! I found it right next to the package, here on your desk!"

"I have no idea what you're talking about,"

Ms. Barbour insisted.

"I'll show you," I said. I hurried back to my desk and riffled through my drawers. Where was that piece of paper with the address? I couldn't find it anywhere.

"I'm sorry, Ms. Barbour," I said when I returned to her office. "I lost the slip of paper with the address on it. But I swear, I never saw an Ocean Drive address."

She frowned, and I realized that the more I said, the sillier I sounded. A slip of paper with the wrong address? It sounded like a lame excuse.

"All right, Mary-Kate," Ms. Barbour said at last. "I drove the posters over to the printer myself first thing this morning. They said they'll rush it and everything will be okay."

That was a relief. So I hadn't ruined everything after all. But I still felt terrible.

"I don't know what happened here," she went on. "But if you're going to work on this Website, I need to be able to rely on you. You'll have to be more careful and responsible from now on—understand?"

"Yes, Ms. Barbour," I said. My face felt hot with embarrassment. I hurried back to my desk.

"Is everything okay?" Stacy whispered to me.

I nodded. I didn't feel like talking about it just then. I tried to work, but it was hard to concentrate.

I don't know how it happened, but I had the wrong address, I thought. But there was no way to prove it.

❀

Mysterio—I'm sorry you didn't like my first match for you. I have to say I was very surprised. Ali is a great girl and I think you should give her a chance. But that's your business, I guess.

I've found two more girls who might make good matches for you. I applied my famous Theory of Compatibility to them and they scored very high with your questionnaire. They both agreed to take a chance on you. Are you willing to take a chance on them?

Both girls go to Bayside High. Caroline Farber is a sophomore and Alicia Gorman is a junior. What do you say, Mysterio?—Ashley

"Want to hit the mall with me after school today, Ashley?" Brittany asked. I was sitting at a computer terminal in the library, getting ready to send my latest E-mail to Mysterio. Brittany read it over my shoulder.

"Sure," I agreed. "I need to buy more film. I've already used up four rolls at Click."

"Wow," Brittany said. "Who knew there were so many kids desperate for dates?"

I turned around to look at her. "They're not desperate," I corrected her. "It's just fun." I turned back to the computer screen and pressed SEND.

Brittany sat on a nearby desk. "Any more clues about this Mysterio guy?" she asked.

I nodded. "I think it's Bart Weinberg."

Brittany stifled a laugh. "Bart Weinberg! Does he even know that girls exist?"

"I guess he does," I said. "Because I spotted a Mysterio sticker on his notebook. So it has to be him!"

Brittany rolled her eyes. "Take a look around, Ashley. Those Mysterio stickers are everywhere!"

I glanced around the library. Brittany was right. In the reading room alone I spotted two boys with Mysterio stickers on their notebooks.

"There's a Mysterio movie coming out soon," Brittany told me. "Haven't you noticed all the Mysterio stuff in the stores? Stickers, posters, action figures—"

"All right, all right," I said. "I guess I'm just not that into comic-book characters."

"And besides," Brittany added, "there's no way, Bart Weinberg is saying no to a date with Ali Riggs."

I sighed. "I know. Bart is probably not Mysterio. It doesn't really make sense. But if it's not him, who is it? It's driving me crazy!"

"Maybe you'll find out today," Brittany said. "When he answers your latest E-mail."

"Hey, Ashley." Somebody tapped me on the shoulder. I turned around.

It was Warren Voigt, Sarah Hunter's old boyfriend.

I'd always liked Warren—he was easygoing and friendly. But at that moment he looked angry.

"Thanks a lot, Ashley," he said. "You've ruined my life!"

chapter nine

"Ruined your life?" I asked Warren. "What are you talking about?"

"You set Sarah up on a date!" Warren yelled. "You broke us up!"

My jaw dropped. I remembered Sarah coming up to me at Click and asking me to fix her up with someone. But she told me that she and Warren had broken up!

I glanced at Brittany, hoping for a little help. But she just shrugged and said, "Um—I've got something to do. See you later, Ashley!" She slinked away, leaving me to face Warren alone.

Coward, I thought.

"I don't understand," I told Warren. "Sarah asked me to find her a date. She told me you two were over!"

Warren slumped against a desk. "I was trying to get back together with her," he said. "It was going really well, too! But last night she went out with *Toby*." He kind of sneered when he said the name. "And now she's going to see him again this weekend! I think she really likes him!"

I felt terrible. Sarah and Warren had been a good couple. But what could I do? If Sarah liked someone else, I couldn't stop her.

"Warren, I'm really sorry," I said. "I had no idea, I swear! What can I do to help you?"

"I'll tell you what you can do," Warren snapped. "You can stay out of my business!"

He stalked away, slamming the library door behind him. Everybody looked up. Their eyes turned toward me.

I shrugged and tried to look innocent. "Um—I guess they didn't have the book he was looking for," I said.

"Ashley!" Paula Cooper stopped me in the hall later that day. I was on my way to check my E-mail before meeting Mary-Kate and Lauren for lunch. Paula was a small, cute girl with long red hair and a high-pitched voice.

I stopped. "Hey, Paula. What's up?"

"He stood me up, that's what!" Paula squeaked. "I was supposed to meet Paul Logan for pizza last night and he never showed up!"

"You're kidding!" I was really surprised. I'd set Paula up on a date with Paul, who went to St. Martin's, a nearby boys' school. He seemed very excited about the date.

"Are you sure there wasn't some mistake?" I asked. "Maybe something happened to him—"

"Nothing happened to him," Paula snapped. "He's just a jerk who didn't feel like showing up! I called him at home to see what the story was, and he was just sitting there, watching TV with his friends!"

"Paula, I'm so sorry—" I began.

"What did you do, fix us up just because our names are Paul and Paula?" Paula demanded. "Did you think that was cute or something?"

"No, really, I didn't," I assured her. "He saw your questionnaire and picture in the notebook and asked me to set up a date with you! It was all his idea, I promise!"

"If it was his idea, why would he stand me up?" Paula asked.

"I don't know," I admitted, and it was true, I couldn't understand it.

"Well, do me a favor—don't bother setting up any more dates for me," Paula grumbled. "I can do better by myself!" She turned and stomped away, her red hair flying behind her.

I took a deep breath and tried to clear my head. This matchmaking business was so much more complicated than I thought. So many things could go wrong!

Maybe Mysterio will cheer me up, I thought as I slipped into the library to check my E-mail. Yes! A message from the mystery boy. Maybe now he'll reveal his identity!

I opened the message from Mysterio.

Sorry, Ashley. I'm not interested in dating Caroline or Alicia. They're both cool girls, but I'm pretty sure they're not right for me. As I said before, I have my reasons. I know I'm being a pain—but will you try again? —Mysterio

I nearly screamed with frustration. He rejected my matches again! Who did this guy think he was?

Maybe he's just toying with me, I thought. *This is getting ridiculous.*

"Ashley, what's the matter?" Mary-Kate asked when I joined her and Lauren at lunch.

"Oh, nothing," I said. "But tell me this—when did everybody in this school get so touchy?"

Lauren laughed. "What are you talking about?"

"Warren Voigt is mad at me because I fixed Sarah up with somebody—and it turns out she likes him," I explained. "Paula Cooper's date stood her up, so now she hates me. And Mysterio rejected two more of my matches!"

"You're kidding!" Mary-Kate exclaimed. "So you still don't know who he is?"

I shook my head. "All I know is he's one picky guy." I sighed. "Let's talk about something else. This matchmaking stuff is starting to make me a little queasy."

"Well, we have to talk about Brittany's birthday party," Lauren said. "It's a week from tomorrow."

"Everyone should have gotten their invitations by now," Mary-Kate reported. "About twenty-five people have gotten back to me so far. Almost everybody's coming."

"We still have to order a cake," I reminded them.

"We'd better do that today," Lauren said. "Let's go to the Cakery. Brittany loves their cakes."

"All right," I agreed. "We'll go this afternoon."

"I can't," Mary-Kate said. "I've got work to do on the Website. I want to prove to Ms. Barbour that I'm responsible. She was really mad when I didn't show up at the printer the other day. I just can't figure out what happened. . . ."

"It *is* weird," I agreed. "Do you think she made a mistake and left the wrong address for you?"

"I don't know," Mary-Kate said. "It wouldn't be like her to make that kind of mistake. She's very organized." She sighed. "Anyway, I can't go to the bakery this afternoon."

"That's all right," Lauren said. "Ashley and I can go."

A tiny little voice in the back of my mind said, *Wait a minute, Ashley. Didn't you have something else to do this afternoon?* But I couldn't remember anything. So much had happened that day, my head was spinning! And it was only lunchtime!

❀

"Steve Sorkin has quit the Website," Ms. Barbour announced that afternoon. Steve was a senior and one of the main writers. "It conflicted with his swimming practice. So I'll need the rest of you to pick up the slack."

The five of us left on staff had gathered in the front of the Website office. Ms. Barbour spoke to us so seriously, it felt as if we were reporters in a real newsroom.

"Mary-Kate, I know your main responsibilities are design and photography," she went on. "But now that Steve is gone, I'd like you to do some more writing."

I nodded, trying to hide my excitement. I loved to write. I even had a secret notebook of story ideas and essays that I worked on in my free time. Best of all, this was a great chance to show Ms. Barbour she could really count on me.

"Steve was working on two sports stories and an essay about applying to colleges," Ms. Barbour said. "I'd like Joseph and Beth to take over the sports articles. The rest of you can work on essays of your own, something to replace Steve's college piece. It can be about anything you want. If you come up with something good, we'll use it."

I went to my desk and pulled my notebook out of my backpack. I had a couple of ideas in there that would make good articles for the Website, and even some finished essays. One was about remembering how awkward I felt freshman year. Another surveyed the styles of different cliques at school.

Stacy smiled at me. "I've got a great idea for a story," she said, and started typing away on her keyboard.

I paged through my notebook. Then I picked up a pen and started scribbling some ideas. I wrote a short, funny piece about cramming for midterms. I hardly had to think about it—the story seemed to write itself.

I quickly typed up my piece, printed it out, and dropped it in Ms. Barbour's in box.

"Thank you, Mary-Kate," she said. "I'll read it right away."

I returned to my desk and worked on the design for the sports page, but it was hard to concentrate. Every once in a while I glanced up at Ms. Barbour's office. Was she reading my piece right now? What did she think of it?

"Let me just check my E-mail one last time," I said, dragging Lauren toward the library. I couldn't shake the feeling that I was forgetting something.

"You can check it when you get home," Lauren said. "Come on, Ashley. We've got to get to the Cakery before it closes. It's all the way downtown and it's always crowded. And besides, picking out the perfect birthday cake takes time."

"All right." I followed her out to the parking lot. We got into my car and drove downtown to the bakery.

We went inside. "Oooh, look at that one," I said, eyeing a red, strawberry-shaped cake coated in whipped cream. "Yum."

"Brittany is allergic to strawberries," Lauren reminded me. "And anyway, she loves chocolate."

"Who doesn't?" I agreed. We consulted with the cake designer and finally settled on a surfboard-shaped chocolate cake with yellow icing, decorated to look like Brittany's birthday gift.

"That is so cool," I said, studying the designer's sketch.

"It's perfect!" Lauren agreed. "I love the Hawaiian flowers!"

My cell phone rang. I reached into my purse to answer it. I checked the caller ID first. Uh-oh. Brittany!

"Hello?" I said.

"Ashley, where are you?" Brittany demanded. "I've been waiting here an hour!"

Oh, no—I *knew* I was forgetting something! I was supposed to go shopping with Brittany after school! And I totally spaced!

I glanced at Lauren. Brittany sounded really annoyed. *What should I do now?*

chapter ten

Lauren stared at me, wide-eyed. "What's happening?" she whispered.

I shook my head. I couldn't explain just then.

"Don't you remember?" Brittany asked. "I asked you if you wanted to go to the mall with me? And you said yes?"

"Brittany, I'm so sorry," I said. "Something came up, and I forgot. I—uh—I had to leave school right away."

"Why?" Brittany asked. "Is everything all right?"

"Um, actually—" I racked my brain for a good excuse. "Yeah, everything's okay, but, um, Lauren's mom got sick again, and I had to drive Lauren home."

"The pediculosis?" Brittany asked.

"Yeah, that's right." I was relieved that Brittany remembered the word, because I'd forgotten it. "Mrs.

Glazer's pediculosis flared up again. But she's much better now. Why don't I come meet you right now?"

"Forget it," Brittany said. "It's too late. I'm going home."

"See you at Click tomorrow?" I asked, but she'd already hung up.

❀

Ms. Barbour finally came out of her office. *Here she comes,* I thought. My hands were shaking. I knew she liked my photographs, but what did she think of my writing?

She stopped at my desk. "Mary-Kate, I loved your story," she said. "Come into my office for a minute and let's talk."

Yes! She liked it! And she was smiling at me. She seemed to have forgotten all about my mistake of a few days earlier.

Stacy looked up from her computer. I followed Ms. Barbour into her office. She motioned for me to sit down next to her desk.

"You're a wonderful writer, Mary-Kate," Ms. Barbour said. "I'd like you to write some full-length articles if you have time."

"I'd love that!" I said. I could write my own articles and illustrate them with my photos. I wouldn't have to rely on Stacy to do the interviewing or writing for me.

"Good. I think it would be great experience for you."

"Thank you," I said. My ears burned, I was so excited. Ms. Barbour was a professional—and she thought I was really good!

"I'd like you to get to work on your next project right away," Ms. Barbour said. "Do you have any ideas?"

"Actually, I do," I said, excited. "What about a story about sweet sixteen parties? It's a big thing for sophomores and juniors. My sister, Ashley, and I had a great one last summer, but it almost didn't work out. We didn't find a place to hold the party until the very last minute! And now we're planning a surprise party for our friend Brittany."

Ms. Barbour nodded. "I like it. You could approach it from a lot of angles. It could be a funny story about what happened to you at your party, or an advice piece for girls planning their own sweet sixteens . . . or a trend story about the hottest ideas for a cool party."

"Or some combination of the three," I added. "I'll start working on it this weekend."

"Excellent," Ms. Barbour said. "It's a fun idea, just the kind of thing I want for the Website."

I practically flew out of her office. I floated over to my desk. Stacy was packing up her things.

"What did she say?" Stacy whispered to me.

"She liked my story," I whispered back. I grabbed my backpack and got ready to leave.

"I want to hear all about it," Stacy said. "Let's go get a cup of coffee."

We went to Click. "I'm so excited!" I said when we were settled at a window table with our coffees. "I mean, I love taking pictures, but I love writing, too. I just never felt sure I was good at it."

"Ms. Barbour knows what she's talking about," Stacy assured me. "If she says you're a good writer, you are."

"How about you?" I asked. "What are you working on?"

"I'm writing an article," Stacy told me. "I don't want to talk about it until it's finished. I'll probably give it to Ms. Barbour on Monday."

"Did you ask her if she'll write you a recommendation?" I asked.

Stacy nodded. "She said she'd be glad to, but she wants to get to know me better first."

"That makes sense," I said. We finished up our coffees and headed home.

❀

"Why did he do it?" I asked. Mary-Kate, Lauren, Brittany, and I had gathered at Click on Saturday afternoon. They were helping me read through the latest dating questionnaires.

"I mean, why would you bother signing up for a matchmaking service if you keep turning down the matches?" I was talking about Mysterio, of course. The secret of his identity was driving me crazy.

"He's probably just picky," Mary-Kate said. She waved a sheaf of papers in my face. "Look—there are tons of girls here who want to be matched up. Maybe we should keep trying."

"I have an idea," Brittany said. She didn't seem mad at me about standing her up the day before, thank goodness. "Why don't *you* fill out one of your own forms. Then you can apply your super-scientific theory to yourself—and Mysterio."

"Yeah," Lauren agreed. "See what kind of score you get."

"Me?" I protested. "But . . . I don't know who the guy is! What if I don't like him?"

"Ali Riggs was willing to take a chance," Brittany reminded me.

"And what about me?" Mary-Kate said. "You used me as a human guinea pig against my will—and I have a date with Mike Mott tonight!"

"It's only fair, Ashley," Lauren said. "You keep telling Mary-Kate to keep an open mind. You should, too."

"All right," I agreed. "Give me half an hour."

I went off to sit at a table by myself so I could concentrate. I filled out a questionnaire as honestly as I could. Then I took Mysterio's form and compared it to mine.

"Are you finished?" Mary-Kate asked. She and Brittany and Lauren gathered around to see what my score was.

I totaled everything up. Then I showed them the score.

"Oh, wow," Lauren gasped. "You're Mysterio's perfect match!"

chapter eleven

"How do I look?" I asked Ashley. I turned in front of her wearing jeans, a pale blue sweater, and boots. I was in my bedroom on Saturday night, getting ready to go out with Mike Mott.

"Mary-Kate, it's a *date,*" she reminded me. "Don't you think you should put a little effort into it?"

"What are you talking about?" I asked.

"If you're wearing any makeup at all, I can't see it," she replied. "You just bought that new sparkly eye shadow—why don't you put some on?"

"I didn't want to go overboard," I explained. "I mean, I'm meeting Mike at the Dude Ranch." The Dude Ranch was a popular skateboard park near the beach. "It's not exactly the Four Seasons."

"It's still a date," Ashley insisted. "Give Mike a little credit and be your usual cute self."

I looked in the mirror. I looked fine, but not special. Ashley was totally right. What was I thinking?

"I guess I'm kind of dreading this date," I admitted as I put on the new eye shadow. Ashley didn't say anything. She was staring at the ceiling again.

"Ashley!" I scolded. "You're the one who got me into this. The least you can do is help me through it."

"Sorry." She sat up. "Keep an open mind," she recited. "Maybe you'll like him more than you expect."

"You don't even mean that anymore," I complained. "I don't think you care whether I like Mike or not. You're obsessed with Mysterio!"

"You're right," Ashley admitted. "But don't you see how big this is? He's my perfect match! But who is he? I'm almost afraid to find out."

"Ashley, he's only perfect according to your theory," I reminded her. "Which is not exactly nuclear physics."

"Are you saying you doubt the theory?" Ashley said, knowing perfectly well what the answer was.

"Well, your theory matched me and Mike Mott," I replied. "So I'll let you know when I get home tonight."

I presented my freshly made-up face for inspection.

"Much better," she said. "Try and have a good time."

"I will." I picked up my fringed leather bag and headed for the Dude Ranch.

"Wicked switchback grab!" I cheered as Mike sailed down a half-pipe, floated into the air, and grabbed his skateboard. I had picked up a little lingo in the half hour I'd been watching Mike. I had to admit, he was pretty good.

He skated up to the bleachers where I sat and flipped his board into the air, catching it and cradling it under one arm.

"Thanks, Mary-Kate," he said. "You want to get something to eat?"

"Definitely," I agreed. "Where should we go?" I couldn't imagine what kind of restaurant a guy like Mike would take me to.

"Ever been to Stoker's?" he asked. "Their pizza's good."

"Really?" I said. "I've never tried it." Now I had my answer. Stoker's wasn't a restaurant at all. It was basically a video arcade that served pizza and burgers.

Not exactly the most romantic spot in the world, I thought. But maybe that was a good thing.

"Come on," Mike said, dropping his board. "You'll love it."

I walked along beside him while he skated slowly down the street.

"Hey, look!" Mike cried when we walked into Stoker's. "The Pulverizer is open! You save it while I go get us a couple of slices."

I leaned against the Pulverizer, a large video game, and waited for Mike to come back.

"Hope you like pepperoni," Mike said when he returned with the pizza. He handed me a slice and a Coke.

"Thanks," I said. I bit into the pizza. I was surprised—it was pretty good.

Mike pumped quarters into the video game. "Ladies first," he offered as the game set up.

"You go first," I said. "I'll watch and finish my pizza." I had no idea how to play Pulverizer, so I wanted to see how it was done.

"Wicked. Let's rip it up," he said. I watched closely as Mike played the game. You had to guide a souped-up car past different obstacles—first a maze full of electric shocks, then some metal-chomping monsters, then some giant apes who shot laser beams at you. If you messed up, the car got smashed by the Pulverizer, sort of a huge crushing machine come to life.

"Dude! I slammed on that last run." Mike's car got pulverized. "Your turn."

I stepped up to the machine. I was glad the game featured a car. If there was one thing I loved, it was driving.

I started my car and steered it through the maze.

"Watch that curve!" Mike coached. "Oh! Nice move. Don't bail—you're doing good!"

I managed to drive my car all the way up to the last row of giant apes before I got pulverized.

"You got a Pulverizer at home?" Mike asked me. "Because you're like a pro at it."

I laughed. "Me? I've never played before."

"No way!" He grinned. "I'm going to kick your butt this round."

"Take your best shot." I moved away to let him take another turn. He did better this time, but I made it all the way to the Ultimate Round, where you have a chance to pulverize the Pulverizer.

"You must be a sick driver," Mike said. "Another round?"

"Why don't we get out of here," I suggested. The electronic game noises were starting to get to me. "Maybe take a walk or something?"

"Okay," Mike agreed. We left the arcade and headed for the boardwalk. We stopped at a stand and bought milk shakes. Then we sat on a bench and watched the in-line skaters flash by.

"So, what are you into?" Mike asked. "I mean, besides school or whatever."

"I love photography," I told him. "And I'm working on the school's new Website. I'm designing it and doing some writing for it."

"Yeah, I heard about that," Mike said. "It sounds excellent. Some girl was asking me and my friends about skater gear."

"That was probably Stacy," I said.

"I've got to tell you something," Mike said. He paused, slurping his shake. "I think you're a really cool girl. But I don't know if I really want a girlfriend or anything right now. I'm totally into skating. I want to turn pro after I graduate."

I tried not to let my relief show on my face. "Don't worry," I said. "I'm really busy now, too, with the Website and everything."

"It's not that I thought you wanted to be my girlfriend," Mike said. "I mean, I don't know what a cool girl like you is doing on a date with me, anyway."

He didn't look shyly away as I thought he would. He looked right at me, his face open and honest. I couldn't help liking him. He would have made a good brother.

"Why did you sign up for the matchmaking service if you don't want a girlfriend?" I asked.

"My friends dared me," he admitted. "They bet me that nobody would go out with me. And then I got matched with you—it was like, whoa." He grinned. "My friends couldn't believe it. *I* couldn't believe it."

"Why not?" I asked.

"I mean, come on," he said. "You're a total babe! When would I get another chance to go out with a girl like you?"

I laughed. I had no idea he even knew who I was before.

"Why *did* you decide to go out with me?" Mike asked. "This isn't a joke or anything, is it? You're not laughing at me behind my back, are you?"

"No!" I assured him. "Not at all. Actually, my sister matched us up. She has this theory. . . . It's too complicated to go into right now. But anyway, she thought we'd be a good match. I told her I wasn't really looking for a boyfriend. But she thought it would look bad for her matchmaking service if her own sister didn't use it."

Mike nodded. "Totally." He tossed his paper cup into the trash. "Hey, I'm glad your sister pushed you into this," he said. "If she hadn't, I never would have found out how cool you are."

I smiled. "I'm glad, too—for the same reason."

❀

"He's not a bad guy," Mary-Kate said. We were hanging out at Click on Sunday afternoon—me, Mary-Kate, Brittany, and Lauren. Mary-Kate was telling us about her date with Mike Mott.

"But he's kind of immature," she added. "All he wants to do is skate and play video games."

"Not really your type," Brittany put in.

Mary-Kate shook her head. "No. So much for your famous theory, Ashley."

"Hey! You and Mike got a good score, not a perfect score," I protested. "And you did *kind of* like him, right? I mean, as a friend."

"Yes," Mary-Kate admitted. "But—"

"So maybe my theory does work," I insisted. "It just needs to be fine-tuned a little."

"If you're so sure your theory works, why don't you use it yourself?" Brittany said.

"You and Mysterio got a perfect score," Lauren chimed in. "Why won't you submit yourself to him as a possible match?"

"I just wish I knew who he was first," I said. "I've asked everybody I can think of. Nobody has a clue!"

"It's time to take a chance, Ashley," Mary-Kate said.

"Let me try to fix him up with someone else—just one more time," I pleaded. "If he bites, at least the mystery will be solved."

"But what if he ends up liking the girl you match him with?" Lauren said. "You'll have missed your chance for true love!"

"It's a risk I'll have to take," Ashley said. "I'm going to try once more."

I already had a couple of girls in mind to suggest to Mysterio—and they'd both already agreed. I went across the room to one of the computer terminals in the back of the café and E-mailed Mysterio. I was starting to feel kind of cranky about his little game. Why couldn't he reveal his identity like everybody else?

Dear Mysterio—I'm giving you one last chance. Make that two last chances. I submit to you Krista Kelly and Anne LaMonica. They are both great girls. You should feel lucky that anyone still wants to go along with this. Think about it and let me know soon. —Ashley

❀

"Mom isn't up to cooking, so Dad's going to make his famous Thai noodles with shrimp," Brittany was saying when I returned to the table.

"Brittany was just telling us what's on the menu this Friday," Lauren explained to me.

"Oh, right," I said to Brittany. "Your birthday."

"Be at my house at six," Brittany said. "It'll be a small but special sweet sixteen."

"Sounds like fun." I tried not to look at Mary-Kate or Lauren. I was afraid one glance would give our surprise away. We'd have a nice quiet dinner at Brittany's house on Friday night—and a huge blowout party on Saturday!

"Did you write to Mysterio?" Lauren asked.

I nodded. "I hope he gets back to me soon. The suspense is killing me!"

I had to stop myself from checking my E-mail five minutes later. *Give the guy a chance,* I thought. *Wait until tonight.*

But as we were leaving the café, I couldn't help myself. "Let me just check my E-mail before we go," I said.

"He probably hasn't even read your message yet," Brittany protested.

"It will just take a second." I punched up my school E-mail account. Luckily, we could access it from anywhere.

"Hey, look!" I called. "I've got mail! And it's from him!"

Mary-Kate, Brittany, and Lauren hurried over to read the message. I opened it.

Dear Ashley—You're right—Krista and Anne are great girls. Really! But I'm not looking for just a date. I'm looking for the perfect girl for me. I know it's going to be hard to find her. Please don't give up on me yet.—Mysterio

"Wow," Mary-Kate gasped. "He rejected your matches again!"

"Ugh!" I groaned. "What does this guy want?"

"Stacy!" Ms. Barbour exclaimed, bursting out of her office. "Your piece is just wonderful! Where did you get such a clever idea? It's perfect for our site!"

I had just walked into the Website office after school on Monday and settled at my desk. I grinned at Stacy. I was glad Ms. Barbour liked her work, too. The Website was going to be awesome!

Stacy shrugged and smiled modestly. "Oh, I don't know where my ideas come from," she said. She stood up and started gathering her things. "I'd better run. I've got to interview the girls' basketball coach. See you tomorrow."

"See you," I said.

"Excellent job, Stacy," Ms. Barbour called after her. Then she turned to me. "Mary-Kate, I'd like you to proofread Stacy's article before we post it on the site. I want you to read it, anyway. It's a great example of the kind of writing you should all be doing."

"Sure, Ms. Barbour," I said. I punched up Stacy's article on my computer and read the title. "Preppie, Surfer, Goth, or Punk? Do You Fit in with the Cliques at Bayside High?"

I gasped. Those were the exact words I had written in my notebook. Stacy had stolen one of my ideas!

chapter twelve

I read on. Stacy hadn't just stolen my idea—she'd ripped off the whole piece!

I felt as though someone had punched me in the stomach. How could Stacy do this to me? I thought she was my friend.

I scanned the article again, just to make sure there was no mistake. I recognized every sentence of it. She'd hardly changed a word.

My notebook. She must have seen my notebook somehow.

I couldn't let Stacy get away with this. I ran after her.

"Stacy!" I called, spotting her down the hall. "Wait!"

She turned and stopped. "I don't have time to talk," she said. "I'm in a hurry."

"I just looked at your latest article," I told

her. "You stole it from me! How could you do that?"

"I don't know what you're talking about," Stacy said. "Are you trying to take credit for my work?"

My jaw dropped open. I couldn't believe her nerve!

"You know that's not true," I insisted.

"Look, I don't have time for this." Stacy turned and walked quickly away.

All right, I thought, gathering my courage. *I tried to reason with her. It didn't work. Now I've got to take the next step.*

I went back to the Website room and marched into Ms. Barbour's office.

"Um, Ms. Barbour," I began. "I think there's been a mistake."

"Yes?"

I felt awkward. I didn't want to accuse Stacy of stealing from me. But what other explanation was there?

"It's about Stacy's clique piece," I said. "That was my idea."

"What do you mean?" Ms. Barbour asked.

"I keep a notebook of writing ideas," I explained. "I had a story in there about cliques, just like Stacy's."

Ms. Barbour pursed her lips. "Mary-Kate, you may have had a similar idea. That happens. But

Stacy did a wonderful job, and you shouldn't try to take that away from her."

"I'm not!" I insisted. "I didn't just have a similar idea. I wrote that article!"

She frowned. "Mary-Kate, Stacy turned in another article today, in the same writing style. So I'm inclined to believe that she is the author of both pieces."

She plucked an article off her desk and handed it to me. I stared at it. "Fitting in as a Freshman—One Girl's First Year of High School."

"I don't believe it!" I gasped. "I wrote this too!"

Ms. Barbour stared at me. "Mary-Kate, do you realize what you're saying?"

"Yes, I do." I was fuming. "Stacy stole both of these stories from me—and I can prove it."

I hurried to my desk. I had to find my notebook. I searched my backpack, but it wasn't there. Then I realized that I probably left it on my desk last Friday.

I searched my desk. No sign of the notebook. It was gone!

I glanced at the open door of Ms. Barbour's office. I could go in there and accuse Stacy of stealing my notebook without proof. But Ms. Barbour didn't seem to have much patience for that.

Or I could go home and think of a way to catch Stacy.

I went home.

"Ashley, just do it!" Brittany urged me. "E-mail Mysterio and suggest yourself as a match for him. It might be the only chance you have of finding out who he is."

"But what if it doesn't work?" I complained. "What if he rejects me like he has everyone else?"

"Then you'll just give up on him," Lauren suggested. "Tell him he's too picky and you can't help him."

"But then I'll never know who he is!" I wailed. "Or what this whole thing was about."

The three of us were lounging in my bedroom on Monday afternoon. Mary-Kate was still at school, working on the Website.

"You're not the only one who's dying of suspense, you know," Brittany snapped. "If you don't do it, I will!"

"Okay, okay," I agreed. "I'll do it." I sat at my desk and logged onto my computer. I was very nervous. Now that I knew Mysterio was my perfect match, I was more eager than ever to find out who he was. But I also knew that if he turned out to be a dud, I'd be very disappointed. And if he didn't want to go out with me, it would hurt—just a little.

I typed:

Mysterio—I've got one more match to offer you. I'm attaching my own questionnaire and photo to this E-mail. When I applied my theory to our forms, we got a very high score. Please let me know your answer right away.—Ashley

❀

I sent the E-mail. "That's it," I said, leaning back in my chair. "Now all we have to do is wait."

"I'm so mad, I could kick the stuffing out of this pillow!" Mary-Kate cried. She came home just before dinner and stormed into my room. She picked up a pillow and drop-kicked it against the wall.

"What's the matter?" I asked. I'd never seen Mary-Kate so furious. I turned away from my computer and sat beside her on the bed. Brittany and Lauren had gone home. I'd been checking my E-mail every ten minutes—still no answer from Mysterio.

"Stacy Segal stole my writing notebook!" Mary-Kate explained. "She copied two stories from it and turned them in to Ms. Barbour, claiming she wrote them! And Ms. Barbour believes her!"

"Just show her your notebook," I suggested. "That will prove that you wrote the stories first."

"I can't!" Mary-Kate said. "It's gone. I bet Stacy has it."

"She's back-stabbing you!" I gasped.

"I know." Mary-Kate sighed. "And now that I think about it, it's not the first time. Remember when Ms. Barbour wanted me to take those posters to the printer? I think Stacy might have taken the address off Ms. Barbour's desk and left me the wrong one."

"She's evil!" I declared. "But why is she doing this?"

"I don't know," Mary-Kate said. "She's a good writer. She doesn't need to steal ideas from me."

"She must be jealous of you," I said. "Ms. Barbour keeps talking about how talented you are. Stacy probably wants to impress her, too."

"Stacy really looks up to Ms. Barbour," Mary-Kate said. "And she wants to get a recommendation from her for college."

"This girl is seriously out to get you," I said. "You've got to stop her."

"But how?" Mary-Kate said. "Without my notebook, I have no way of proving that I wrote those pieces. Ms. Barbour must think *I'm* the one trying to take credit for *Stacy's* ideas!" She covered her face with her hands and fell back against the pillows.

"Very simple," I said. "You have to set a trap for her. And I know how."

chapter thirteen

"Hi, Stacy," I said as I walked into the Website office the next afternoon. I acted as if nothing had happened. I was curious to see how she'd react.

"Hi," she said stiffly. She acted as if she were concentrating very hard on something on her computer screen.

I don't believe it, I thought as I sat at my desk. *She's acting as if she's mad at me!*

I was dying to confront her again. I wanted to demand my notebook back. But I knew she'd only deny everything.

Stick to the plan, I told myself. *Be patient and stick to the plan.*

Ms. Barbour came in a few minutes later. "Hello, girls," she said. "I'm in my office if you need me." She breezed into her office and shut the door.

I wanted to burst into her office and say, "Stacy is stealing my ideas—and I can prove it!" But I needed a day or two for Ashley's plan to work. So I didn't say anything. No reason to stir up trouble.

I started working on an article about sweet sixteen parties—the idea I'd mentioned to Ms. Barbour the week before. I threw myself into the writing. I had no idea how much time passed. But when I looked up, Stacy and the others were gone for the day. Only Ms. Barbour and I were left.

My article was finished. I saved it and printed out two copies and took one of them to Ms. Barbour.

"Here's that sweet sixteen piece I was working on," I said.

"Thank you, Mary-Kate," Ms. Barbour said. "I'll read it tonight." She paused, glancing at her calendar. I started to leave, but she called me back.

"The girls' basketball team has a big game this afternoon," she told me. "I think we ought to cover it—and I'd like you to shoot a few photos of the game. Okay?"

"No problem," I said. "I'll stop by the office after the game."

"Good. See you tomorrow."

Before I left for the day, I slipped the second copy of my article under a few papers on my desk to make it look as if I was still working on it.

The trap is set, I thought. *Let's see if she takes the bait.*

❀

"Any word from Mysterio yet?" Mary-Kate asked me. It was almost lunchtime, and I bumped into her on the way to the cafeteria. She and I had been glued to the computer the night before, checking my E-mail every two seconds, but Mysterio never wrote.

"I was just about to stop into the library and check," I told her. "For the fiftieth time today."

We went into the library and sat down at a computer terminal. I took a deep breath and clicked open my mail. Yes! A reply from Mysterio!

"Open it!" Mary-Kate urged.

The message was very short. *Ashley—You've finally found someone I'm interested in. You.*

chapter fourteen

"He likes you!" Mary-Kate squealed. "Maybe your theory really does work!"

My heart was racing. "Maybe," I said. "But I still don't know who he is."

"Write him back and ask," Mary-Kate said. "He told you he would reveal his identity when you matched him with someone he liked. He *has* to do it now!"

I clicked REPLY and started writing back to Mysterio. *I'm glad you're finally interested in one of my matches. But you promised to reveal your identity. Who are you?*

I waited a few anxious minutes. Mary-Kate nervously tapped her knee. "What if it turns out to be someone you don't like?" she asked. "Or someone at school who you've never met before? Or someone you're friends with?"

"Stop it, Mary-Kate," I said. "You're making me even more nervous! We'll find out in a minute, okay?"

Mysterio IM'd back. *I'll call you tonight. Then you'll know who I am. If you don't want to go out with me when you find out, I'll understand. I won't hold you to it.*

"Ugh!" I groaned in frustration. "Why does he have to keep dragging this out?"

"Bayside wins!" the announcer shouted. The fans flooded the basketball court, celebrating with the girls' team. "Next stop, the state conference championships!"

I snapped pictures of the happy players jumping up and down and hugging one another. This will be a great story for the Website. The Bayside High girls' basketball team was going to the championships for the first time ever.

I took photos of the stands emptying onto the court, the fans cheering, the losing team looking dejected. I got a few shots of the team surrounding their coach and heading for the locker room. Then I hurried back to the Website office to write about the game.

"We won!" I announced as I walked into the office. Joseph and Beth, two seniors who wrote for the site, sat huddled together, whispering. Joseph looked up and me and put his finger to his lips.

"Shhh," he whispered. He nodded toward Ms. Barbour's office. "She's on a rampage. Stacy's in there."

The door to Ms. Barbour's office was closed. I could see the back of Stacy's head through the window.

"What's going on?" I asked.

"We don't know," Beth said. "Stacy gave Ms. Barbour an article about half an hour ago. Then Ms. Barbour came out of her office and called Stacy in. Her face was all red. She looked really mad."

"They've been in there for about ten minutes," Joseph added.

I riffled through the papers on my desk. Aha. The copy I'd made of my sweet sixteen article was gone.

I had a feeling I knew what was going on in that office.

The office door opened and Ms. Barbour stepped out. "Is Mary-Kate back yet?" she asked. Before anyone had a chance to answer, she spotted me at my desk. "Please come in here, Mary-Kate," she said.

Joseph and Beth looked nervous for me as I headed for the office. "Good luck," Beth whispered.

I took a deep breath and stepped into the office. "Close the door," Ms. Barbour ordered.

"Stacy turned this article in this afternoon." She passed me a few pieces of paper. I tried not to smile as I read the title—"Happy Birthday! Sixteen Sweet Ideas for Celebrating Your Sweet Sixteen."

The trap worked. Stacy fell for it hook, line, and sinker.

"Stacy's article matches the one you gave me almost word for word," Ms. Barbour says. "Can you explain this?"

"Yes," I replied. "I wrote this article, and Stacy copied it."

"That's a lie!" Stacy cried. "I was working on this story all week. Mary-Kate found it in my desk. *She* copied it!"

I stared at her, amazed. How could she lie like that right to my face? When she knew that I knew the truth!

"This article is written in the same style as Stacy's other recent pieces," Ms. Barbour said. "I'm inclined to believe her on this."

What? "That's because she copied the other pieces from me, too!" I explained. "And I can prove it! Follow me."

I marched out of the office, straight for Stacy's desk. Beth and Joseph stared at us, wide-eyed.

"Open your desk drawers, Stacy," I demanded. "Let's see what's in there."

Stacy smirked at me. "Okay," she said. She slid open the drawers. Inside were some magazines and papers—including my copy of the sweet sixteen article.

"There!" I cried, picking up the article. "I left this on my desk last night—and now it's gone! She took it and copied it!"

"No I didn't," Stacy insisted. "I made that copy for myself."

"I can prove that I wrote it first," I said. "I saved it on my computer. The date and time are recorded there."

I punched up my files and showed Ms. Barbour the date and time of the article.

"What about you, Stacy?" Ms. Barbour asked. "Can you show me that you saved this story earlier?"

Stacy looked nervous. "These computer clocks aren't always accurate," she said.

Ms. Barbour glared at her. "Stacy, please open your files."

Her fingers shaking, Stacy opened her documents. There was the article—saved a day later than mine. Ms. Barbour's face got red. She looked at Stacy.

"Stacy, come with me," she said grimly.

Stacy followed Ms. Barbour into her office. The door closed. A few minutes later the door flew open and Stacy ran out. She stuffed her things into her backpack and dashed out of the room, crying.

I felt sad for her. She was a good writer. She should have believed in her own talent and not worried so much about getting Ms. Barbour's approval.

"May I see you please, Mary-Kate?" Ms. Barbour beckoned.

I went into the office and sat down. "I'm sorry I doubted you," Ms. Barbour said. "I asked Stacy to leave the Website. I won't tolerate plagiarism."

I nodded. I wasn't sure what to say.

"I had no idea Stacy was so dishonest," she continued. "But your work is excellent. You should be very proud of it."

"Thank you."

"With Stacy gone, that leaves more work for the rest of us," she added. "I'm going to ask you to do even more writing now than before. But I think you can handle it."

I smiled. "I'm sure I can."

"Your sweet sixteen piece is wonderful," she added. "I definitely want to use it. And I'd like to illustrate it with one of the photos I saw at the art show—the group shot of you and your friends at your birthday party. How does that sound?"

"Great!" I replied. I remembered the photo she meant—a very happy picture of me, Ashley, Brittany, and Lauren, all dressed up and smiling.

"Good." Ms. Barbour smiled, and the anger drained from her face. "I apologize again," she said. "But now the drama is over, and it's time to get back to work!"

I went back to my desk and let out a breath. Then I began to write.

❀

"Wow, that Stacy's got nerve," I said that evening. Mary-Kate was telling me all about the showdown at the Website. We were sitting in my room after dinner, waiting for Mysterio's phone call.

"I know," Mary-Kate said. "I wasn't sure our plan would work. I mean, she must have known that if she kept copying my stuff, she'd get caught eventually."

"You should take it as a compliment," I told her. "She obviously thinks you're a great writer or she wouldn't have done it."

The phone rang. I jumped. Mary-Kate stared at it as if it were about to explode.

"This is it," I said. "We're about to find out Mysterio's identity at last!"

"Answer it!" Mary-Kate cried.

I picked up the phone. "Hello?"

"Hello, Ashley? This is Mysterio."

chapter fifteen

"Mysterio's voice sounded familiar. But I still couldn't tell who he was. "Who are you?" I asked. "Do I know you?"

"Yes," Mysterio said. "I'm in your art class. Aaron Moore."

I nearly dropped the phone on the floor. Aaron Moore! The cutest guy in school! It couldn't be him. He was the last person to need a matchmaker.

Mary-Kate tugged on my sleeve. "Who is it? Who is it?" she whispered.

I covered the receiver with my hand. "He says he's Aaron Moore."

Her jaw dropped. "Aaron Moore? No way!"

"Ashley? Are you there?" Aaron asked.

"Sorry," I said.

"Are you disappointed?" he asked. "You don't have to go out with me if you don't want to."

The more I listened to his voice, the more I recognized it. It *was* Aaron. Aaron Moore was Mysterio!

"No, I'm not disappointed at all," I replied. "I'd love to go out with you." I paused. I still had so many questions.

"Aaron, can I ask you something?" I began.

"Sure," he said.

"Why did you sign up for the matchmaking service?" I inquired. "You're always going on tons of dates. You don't need any help with that."

"I know," he said. "I've dated a lot of girls. Actually, I'd already been out with every girl you tried to match me with—except you."

I laughed. "So that's how you knew they weren't right for you!"

"Yeah," he admitted. "The thing is, I don't want to go on a lot of dates. I'm looking for a girlfriend. But I couldn't seem to find the right girl on my own. I was hoping your Theory of Compatibility would work for me."

Wow! Maybe my theory actually worked! "But why didn't you want anyone to know your identity?" I asked.

"Well. . ." He paused, sounding uncomfortable. "Sometimes I feel like I attract the wrong kind of girl. Girls like me for the way I look or because I've got a lot of friends. They don't even bother to really get to know me."

I smiled to myself. He was trying to find a modest way of saying girls liked him because he was cute.

"So if they saw my picture in your dating book and knew it was me, I'd just end up with more of the same type of girl," he finished. "But if someone read my questionnaire and liked the answers on it without knowing what I looked like, then they might be interested in the real me."

I had to admit I'd misjudged Aaron. I thought he was just a girl magnet. I never realized he was deeper than that.

"So, Ashley, now that you know who I am, do you still want to go out with me?"

"I'd love to, Aaron," I replied. I couldn't wait!

"How about this weekend?" he asked.

"I can't do it this weekend," I said. "I'm planning a surprise party for Brittany. It's on Saturday afternoon at Click. You can come if you want. Be there before three. That's when Brittany arrives."

"Sounds good. So maybe next weekend?"

"Next weekend would be excellent," I agreed.

"Cool," he said. "I can't wait. And Ashley—thanks for your help. I have a feeling your theory will work out great for me."

My whole body tingled as I hung up the phone. "I can't believe it," I said to Mary-Kate. "My perfect match is Aaron Moore!"

"Aaron Moore is Mysterio?" Brittany gasped. "You're not serious."

"It's true," Ashley told her.

"I was there when he called," I said. "I can vouch for it."

We were sitting in the cafeteria with Brittany and Lauren on Thursday afternoon. Brittany's birthday party was only two days away. Ashley, Lauren, and I still had a lot to do to set up the surprise—including getting Brittany to Click for the party.

But Ashley's news about Aaron was too big—it couldn't wait.

"He's so cute," Lauren said. "And he wants *you* to be his girlfriend! It's so exciting!"

"Whoa, wait a second." Ashley made a "hold it" gesture with her hand. "We haven't even been on a date yet. And we don't know each other that well."

"But you're his perfect match!" Lauren protested.

"Yeah, Ashley," I teased. "Your theory said so. Don't tell me you doubt the theory?"

"I still believe in the theory," Ashley insisted. "But I can't say it's one hundred percent foolproof."

"So, are you going out with him this weekend?" Brittany asked.

"Next weekend," Ashley replied. "But speaking of this weekend, Mary-Kate heard about a beach party on Saturday."

I nodded. "Some guy who goes to Westside High is having a huge beach party Saturday afternoon. You guys want to go?"

"Definitely," Brittany said. "What time?"

"Why don't we all go together?" Lauren said.

"Good idea," I said. "Let's meet at Click at three."

"I'm there," Brittany agreed.

I sneaked a glance at Ashley. When Brittany walked into Click on Saturday afternoon—surprise! It was going to be great!

❀

"The Website will be up on the Web next week," Ms. Barbour announced after school that day. I cheered along with Joseph, Beth, and the other staff members—except for Stacy, of course.

"I want to thank you all for your hard work," Ms. Barbour added. "We got this off the ground in record time—and it's going to be a hit with the students, I'm sure."

We all cheered again. Ms. Barbour nodded at Joseph, who picked up a stack of posters. "This afternoon Joseph will plaster the school with these posters advertising the site." She held up one of the posters. It was slickly designed and in colorful letters were the words, "Want the real

411? Log on. Don't be left out of the loop." Then it gave the Website address.

"Okay, back to work, everyone," Ms. Barbour said. "And thanks again. We'll celebrate next week when the site goes up."

She disappeared into her office. I went back to proofreading a piece Beth wrote. My cell phone rang.

"Hey, Mary-Kate." It was Ashley. "Lauren and I are picking up the party decorations, but we need someone to call the caterers and give them the final head count. Will you be working much longer?"

"I'm almost finished for the day," I told her, flipping through my appointment book. "I'll call the caterers' before I go home. Any word on the surfboard?"

"It won't be ready until tomorrow afternoon," Ashley reported. "We'll have to drive down to Huntington Beach and pick it up after school."

"Wait a second," I said. "Brittany's birthday dinner is tomorrow night at six. How can we drive all the way to Huntington Beach and be back in time for the dinner?"

Ashley sighed. "You're right. And there won't be time to drive down there Saturday morning—we have too much to do! We've got to pick up the cake, decorate the café, set up the food—"

"But Brittany will kill us if we're late for her birthday dinner," I put in. "And we can't tell her why we're late—it will ruin the surprise!"

"How about this," Ashley said. "You and Lauren drive down to Huntington Beach to get the board tomorrow. If you hurry, you can be back by six-thirty. In the meantime, I'll go to Brittany's house at six and stall her."

"Good," I said. "We'll call you if we're running late, and you can make up some kind of excuse for us. But at least she won't be left all alone on her birthday!"

"Right," Ashley said. "Okay—good plan. We've got to keep cool. We don't want to do anything that will give away the surprise."

"Brittany has no clue about the party," I said. "She's going to be blown away!"

"Happy birthday, Brittany!" I said.

It was six o'clock on Friday night, Brittany's official birthday. I stood on her doorstep, hiding a small package behind my back. It was a decoy present—a couple of CDs. Brittany would think it was weird if I showed up empty-handed on her birthday. She had no idea that the next day she'd be getting a customized surfboard!

"Thanks, Ashley," Brittany said. "Come on in. Where's Mary-Kate?"

"She'll be here soon," I said. "She probably had a few last-minute things to do on the Website."

Brittany led me into the living room. Through a glass door I glimpsed the deck, where a table was beautifully set for Brittany's birthday dinner.

"I wonder where Lauren is, too," Brittany said. "I thought she'd come over early to help me set up. But I haven't heard from her all afternoon."

"I'm sure she'll be here soon," I said. I held out the decoy present. "Here—happy birthday."

"Thank you!" She took the package. "Can I open it now?"

"Go ahead," I said. It would use up a little time.

Brittany tore open the wrapping paper. "Link Ray's *Surf Guitar*!" she cried, holding up a CD. "Thanks, Ashley—I've wanted to get this for a long time."

She went to the stereo and put it on. "Want some iced tea?" she offered. "Or lemonade?"

"Iced tea sounds good," I said. I followed her into the kitchen. She fixed two glasses of iced tea and got a bowl of chips and dip.

"We're having Dad's special Thai noodles for dinner," Brittany told me. "Everything's ready—he just has to stir-fry the noodles and we can eat."

"Yum," I said. I glanced at the clock. Six-thirty. Where were Lauren and Mary-Kate?

Brittany and I took our drinks out on the deck. The sun was setting, so Brittany lit some candles and tiki torches.

"It's beautiful out here," I told her.

"Thanks." She sat down and glanced at her watch. "Where are they?" she asked. "I can't believe they'd be late for my birthday!"

I shifted in my seat. "I know—isn't it weird? Something must have come up. You know they'd never be late on purpose."

Brittany frowned. "I don't know—I've been feeling kind of insecure lately. You and Mary-Kate and Lauren have always been such good friends. I could always count on you. But lately—" She paused. "You've all been acting weird—standing me up, and doing things without me—"

I couldn't stand to hear anymore. "Brittany, you've got it all wrong. We love you!"

She looked at her watch again. "So, then, where are they? It's almost seven. They're an hour late!"

My cell phone rang. I reached into my purse. "This is probably Mary-Kate now," I said, clicking the phone on. "Hello?"

"Ashley, it's me. Mary-Kate."

"Where are you?" I asked. I had to be careful not to say anything that would give away the truth to Brittany.

"We've got the board," Mary-Kate told me. "It's gorgeous! But we're stuck on the highway—

the traffic is brutal! We should have known not to try this on a Friday night."

I sighed. "When can you get here?"

"I have no idea," Mary-Kate said. "I guess we're at least forty-five minutes from home."

Great. What was I going to do? "Get here as soon as you can," I told her and hung up.

Brittany gave me her suspicious eyebrows-raised look. "What's going on?" she asked.

I had to think of something fast. Brittany's mother picked that moment to step out onto the deck. "Hi, girls," she said. She was very pregnant. "How's everything going out here?"

"Hi, Mrs. Bowen," I said. I was glad to see her—now I had a few minutes to think. "When is the baby due?"

"Any second now." She smiled and patted her stomach. "Your dinner's almost ready. Where are Mary-Kate and Lauren?"

"Ashley was just about to tell me that," Brittany said.

"Well, Mary-Kate just called," I said, stalling for time. "And she's with Lauren—because, um—" I fell back on the same excuse we'd been using all along. "Lauren's mother got sick again. Mary-Kate went with Lauren to take her to the doctor."

"What a shame," Mrs. Bowen said. "What's the matter with Lauren's mother?"

"She has pediculosis," I explained.

A funny look crossed Mrs. Bowen's face. "Pediculosis?" she said. "You mean head lice?"

My heart sank. Pediculosis was head lice? Oh, no! How was I supposed to know that?

Brittany glared at me. "Are you telling me Lauren's mother has lice? That's the big emergency?"

"Well, um—" I stammered. "Maybe I got it wrong—"

"You didn't get it wrong," Brittany accused. "You've been telling me all along that Mrs. Glazer has head lice. Which is obviously not true. And even if it were true, it's no emergency."

"Well, you know, I guess it can be pretty itchy—"

"You've been lying to me all this time!" Brittany cried. "You and Mary-Kate and Lauren! Why?"

What could I say? I didn't want to give the surprise away—not after all our hard work. Most of all, I didn't want to spoil it for Brittany!

I opened my mouth, but nothing came out. I didn't want to lie anymore—but I couldn't tell the truth.

"Why don't you just go home?" Brittany fumed. "You have ruined my birthday!"

chapter sixteen

"I'll leave you two to talk this out," Mrs. Bowen said. She disappeared into the house.

"Brittany—you don't understand!" I pleaded.

"Explain it to me, then," she demanded.

But I couldn't. More lies would only make things worse.

Brittany stood up. "Go home. And tell Mary-Kate and Lauren not to bother coming."

She stormed into the house. I picked up my bag and followed her.

"What about tomorrow?" I asked. She led me to the front door. "Are we still going to the beach party together?"

"Just leave," Brittany said.

Oh, no, I thought. *What if she doesn't show up at Click tomorrow? How will we get her to the surprise party?*

"Please don't be mad, Brittany," I begged. "I promise you that we all care about you very much."

"When you care about someone, you show up for her birthday dinner on time," she snapped. "I asked you to leave. Now please go home."

I stepped outside and she closed the door.

I stood on her front steps, stunned. What had just happened? How had everything gone so wrong?

I called Mary-Kate on my way home and filled her in.

"Will she show up for the party tomorrow?" Mary-Kate asked.

"I don't know," I replied. "She wouldn't say. She just told me to leave."

"Oh, no," Mary-Kate said. "That doesn't sound good."

"Why did we have to make up those stupid lies about pediculosis?" I wailed. "No wonder she's so upset. We've spoiled everything! We've ruined our best friend's sweet sixteen!"

❀

"Still no answer." Ashley sighed. "I keep getting her voice mail."

It was two o'clock Saturday afternoon. Lauren, Ashley, and I were at Click, setting up Brittany's surprise party. We'd been trying to reach her all morning, but there was no answer at her house and she wasn't picking up her cell phone.

"Did you leave her a message?" I asked.

"I left her a million messages," Ashley said. "On every possible phone, plus E-mail. She's ignoring us! I even called her parents, but there was no answer."

I was desperate to reach her. I had to find a way to make everything up to her and convince her to come to the party. Ashley and I stopped by her house, but no one was home. We couldn't find her anywhere!

"She'll show up—I know it," Lauren insisted.

"Why should she?" I said. "After all we've done to her?"

"Look—here come the first guests!" Ashley said.

Our friends Melanie and Tashema walked into the café, carrying presents. "Surprise!" Melanie yelled.

"I'm so excited!" Tashema squealed. "Does she suspect anything?"

I shook my head. "She has no clue." I didn't want to add that she might not show up at all.

Guests began to trickle in. By two-thirty, almost everyone had arrived, and the party was going strong. Aaron walked in and headed straight for Ashley.

The guests chatted, drinking cold punch and wearing leis around their necks. The café looked beautiful, decorated with wreaths of Hawaiian flowers, pictures of surfers, and a big photo of Brittany catching a wave. The custom surfboard leaned against the back wall, tied with a big blue ribbon. Everything was perfect.

"Hey, everybody," Ashley shouted a little while later. "It's almost three! Brittany will be here any minute!"

"We hope," I added under my breath.

"Everybody hide!" Lauren cried.

We all crowded into the back of the L-shaped room around the corner from the door. Brittany would walk in and think the café was empty. But when she rounded the L—surprise!

A few people whispered and someone shushed them. Next to me, Lauren giggled.

Five minutes passed, then ten.

"Where is she?" someone complained.

"Wait—someone's coming!"

The bell on the front door jangled as it opened. Someone had come into the café. We crouched down and waited.

A shadow loomed across the floor, and someone stepped around the corner.

"Surprise!" we all shouted, jumping up.

"Hey—am I late?" It was only Mike Mott.

Everyone groaned. I grabbed Mike by the arm and led him toward the back wall.

"Yes, you're late," I told him. "We thought you were Brittany."

We pressed ourselves into the back of the room and waited. Half an hour passed. Then an hour. No Brittany.

"She's not coming," Ashley whispered to me. "The party is ruined!"

chapter seventeen

"I can't believe she isn't showing up," Mary-Kate said, looking sad.

"We made our best friend so mad, she probably won't ever speak to us again!" I wailed.

"Can we stop hiding now?" Melanie asked.

I nodded. "Everyone relax. Brittany isn't coming. You might as well enjoy yourselves. The buffet is now open!"

The guests spread out. A few people started eating the snacks and sandwiches we'd spread on a table. But the festive mood was gone.

"Man, what a bummer," Mike Mott said before he stuffed a mini-taco into his mouth.

Aaron waved to me from across the room. He looked like he wanted to come over and talk to me, but two girls had him cornered by the punch.

I slumped into a booth next to Lauren. Mary-Kate came over and joined us.

"I really thought she would come," Lauren said. "I mean, we messed things up, sure . . ."

"We messed up big time," I put in.

"But she knows we care about her no matter what," Lauren said. "How could she not know that?"

"We really screwed up," Mary-Kate said. "We were so busy trying to surprise her that we ended up hurting her feelings!"

"Hey, you guys." Tashema set a plate of sandwiches on our table. "The food's really good. You did a great job."

"Yeah, right." I groaned. "Look at everybody. They're all moping around. This party is a big flop."

Mary-Kate stood up. "We might as well try to have fun if we can. I'm going to put on some music."

She put on a CD of surfing tunes. It didn't perk people up. It only made us think of Brittany.

Aaron finally wrenched himself from the clutches of the other girls and appeared at our table. "Come on, Ashley, cheer up," he said. "Do you want to do the twist?"

An old song from the sixties played. I didn't really feel like dancing. But Aaron offered me his hand, and I couldn't resist. "Let's twist," I said.

"Hey—what's going on?"

It was Brittany!

Everyone stopped for a second and stared at her. Then Lauren jumped up and yelled, "Surprise!"

"Surprise!" we all repeated. I ran across the room and hugged her.

Brittany looked shocked. "What is this?"

"It's a surprise party," I told her. "The most messed-up surprise party ever, until now. Happy sweet sixteen!"

"Where have you been?" Lauren asked. "We've been trying to call you all day!"

"Sorry," Brittany said. "I was at the hospital. My mom just had her baby! I've got a little brother!"

"Congratulations!" I shouted, throwing my arms around her.

Everyone gathered around to congratulate her. The party picked up steam. More people started dancing. Ashley and I led Brittany to a table piled with presents.

"So this is what all the mystery was about," Brittany said, grinning at us. "Head lice! What were you thinking?"

"We were so afraid you wouldn't come," I said. "I thought you were mad at us."

"I was mad," Brittany admitted. "But I know you guys really care about me. I know you wouldn't try to hurt me. And I planned to be here on time, I swear! But then Mom went into labor early this morning. We were at the hospital for hours. I forgot about everything else until it was too late to meet you. But I hoped you guys would still be here, waiting for me."

"And here we were!" Ashley said. "So you really didn't suspect anything?"

"Well—" Brittany smiled. "I wasn't sure. But when your friends have secrets and it's right around your birthday . . . I figured something might be up."

We all laughed. I stood up and said, "Here's something I'll bet you never expected. Come with me."

I took Brittany by the hand and led her to the back of the room. She took one look at the surfboard and shrieked.

"Is it for me?" she asked, touching it gently.

"Who else?" Ashley said. "It says 'Brittany' right here."

"I love it!" Brittany exclaimed. "Thank you so much, all of you. This is the best sweet sixteen ever!"

"Hey, happy birthday, Brittany," Aaron said. "That's a sweet surfboard you've got."

"It's beautiful," Brittany gushed. "I can't wait to try it out."

"Come on, Brittany!" We grabbed Brittany by the hands and pulled her to the dance floor. "It's your birthday! And your baby brother's birthday! Let's celebrate!"

I was so glad Brittany was back. She looked so happy. And the party was the blast we hoped it would be.

❀

Aaron twirled me around on the dance floor one more time and said, "Let's get some punch."

We settled at a table with our drinks. "So are we on for next Saturday night?" he asked me.

"We're on," I said. "What do you want to do?"

"I was thinking I could take you out for an Italian dinner," Aaron said. "I know this place by the beach that makes a wicked shrimp fettuccine."

"Shrimp fettuccine! That's my favorite food," I said.

"I know," Aaron admitted. "You wrote it on your questionnaire."

I laughed and picked up my glass. "Cheers," I said, clinking glasses with him. "I can't wait for next Saturday."

I had a feeling it was going to be the best date of my life.

Find out what happens next in

Sweet 16

Book 8:

CROSS OUR HEARTS

"Let's sit outside, Ashley," Aaron said. He led me to a shady spot under a tree in the courtyard. We leaned against the tree and unpacked our lunches.

"Mmm—my mom makes the best chicken salad," he said through a mouthful of sandwich. "She puts these Indian spices in. Here, have a bite."

He held out the sandwich. I leaned forward and took a bite. It was delicious, with almonds and raisins and curry powder. "That's good," I said.

"Hey guys." Lauren sat down beside us and opened her brown paper lunch bag. "Ashley, do you want to come over to Brittany's house after school today?" she asked me. "She's baby-sitting Lucas and I told her I'd keep her company."

"I can't," I said. "I'm meeting with Ms. Barbour at the Website office this afternoon. I have a great idea for a new column—a matchmaking feature!"

Aaron started laughing. "You're going to put your Click thing on line?"

"Exactly," I said. "You fill out the questionnaire, click on a button, and presto! My theory calculates your perfect match."

"What a great idea," Lauren said. "Can you really do that?"

"Actually, I've got to find somebody to help me program it." I glanced at Aaron.

"Don't look at me," he said. "I can't do anything on the computer unless my little sister shows me how."

"Why don't you ask Malcolm?" Lauren said. "He troubleshoots all the computers at Click."

I paused. I was sure Malcolm would know how to write the program I wanted. I just wasn't sure he'd be willing to help me. He wasn't a big fan of the theory.

"Hey, Moore." Jim Hawley, a friend of Aaron's, stood over us tapping a Frisbee against his knee. "Play a little catch?"

"Definitely." Aaron leaned over and kissed me on the cheek. Then he jumped to his feet and joined his friends on the field.

Lauren watched Aaron toss the Frisbee to his friends. "It's amazing," she said. "Aaron was the guy no girl could catch—and you caught him!"

"Hey, guys." Malcolm joined me and Lauren under the tree. "Excuse me while I barf up my lunch. They call it beef stew. I call it a guaranteed stomachache. Bleh." He leaned over and made fake barfing noises.

Lauren rolled her eyes. "Please, I'm trying to eat here."

"I always pack my own lunch on beef stew days," I said. "You have to check the lunch schedule."

"Remind me to nominate you for a Nobel Prize," Malcolm said. "The Nobel Prize for Excellence in Lunch-Planning. Or should it be Matchmaking?"

He walked right into it. "Speaking of match-making," I began. A look of disgust crossed Malcolm's face, but I didn't let that stop me. "I need a favor, Malcolm. Could you help me set up a matchmaking program on the school Website?"

"I could if I wanted to," Malcolm said. "Unfortunately for you, I don't want to."

"Come on, Malcolm," I begged. "My Theory of Compatibility can bring happiness to hundreds of kids!"

"Misery, you mean."

"It worked great for Ashley," Lauren said.

"And Mary-Kate is interviewing other couples who got together because of the theory too," I said. "Just because you're not into it doesn't mean you shouldn't help me."

"All right, I'll help you," Malcolm agreed. "But will you let me stick some funny bugs in the program? You know, like you click on "FIND MY MATCH" and a skull and crossbones appears? Or maybe a flashing red light that says "Danger! Danger!"

"No," I said. "No, you can't. But if you help me, I'll bring you something yummy for lunch every day for a week. How's that?"

"Better than nothing," Malcolm said. "It's a deal."

❁

"Hello, Kristen? This is Mary-Kate." I was in my room Monday night calling up people who'd used Ashley's matchmaking service at Click. My information said that Ashley had applied her theory to match Kristen Carson with a guy named Bob McSweeney.

"Hi, Mary-Kate," Kristen said. "What's up?"

"I'm doing some research for Ashley," I said. "I see that you filled out a questionnaire at Click a little while ago. So how are things going with Bob McSweeney?"

"You mean Bob McCreepy?" Kristen snapped. "Lousy!"

Click.

"Hello?" I said. It sounded as if she'd hung up on me! But that couldn't be. "Hello?"

No answer. She actually hung up!

I tried a few more people. Stephanie Duarte told me her date got up to go to the bathroom in the middle of dinner and never came back. Bailey Lenhard said her date brought his mother along with him—and turned out to be twelve years old. Oliver Peddy reported that his match was a dog—literally. Some guy had filled out the questionnaire for his dog as a joke.

This is terrible, I thought. *I can't find anyone who found a happy match through Ashley's theory.*

What's going on here? Does the theory work at all?

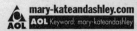

mary-kateandashley

Sweet 16

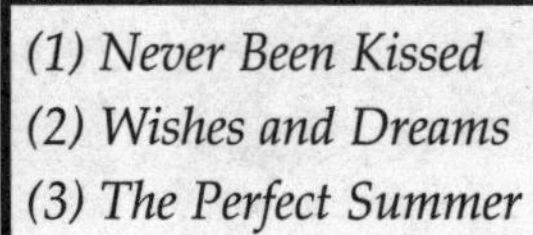

(1) *Never Been Kissed*	(0 00 714879 8)
(2) *Wishes and Dreams*	(0 00 714880 1)
(3) *The Perfect Summer*	(0 00 714881 X)

HarperCollins*Entertainment*

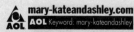